MARIANNE
IN INDIA

and seven other tales

LION FEUCHTWANGER

MARIANNE IN INDIA

and seven other tales

TRANSLATED BY BASIL CREIGHTON

THE VIKING PRESS·NEW YORK
MCMXXXV

Note

Most of the stories collected in this volume were written in the years 1920 to 1928. They were intended to throw light on the background of my novel, *Success*. Three of them, indeed, were included in that work.

When at the beginning of 1933 my home in Berlin was searched by the National Socialists and nearly all my manuscripts, as well as those entrusted to me by friends in other countries, were destroyed, I thought the time had come to collect those of my shorter stories which I could still lay hands on.

L. F.

Contents

MARIANNE
IN INDIA

MARIANNE IN INDIA

By the third week out from Portsmouth, the passengers
on the *Duke of Grafton* had all sniffed at each other and
made friends or the reverse; everybody knew everybody inside out. It was a long voyage to India when you had to sail
round the Cape. It was reckoned nineteen weeks from
Portsmouth to Madras, if all went well; but you might
easily spend six months at sea. They were now off the west
coast of Africa and it was damnably hot. The East India
Company's ships were not of the most comfortable, and
the *Duke of Grafton* was not the most comfortable of the
Company's ships. The lack of comfort was unpleasant and
the heat still more unpleasant; but worst of all was the
boredom.

Besides the ship's complement there were forty-one passengers on board. They were nearly all soldiers, most of
whom were making their first voyage to India; then there
were a few of the Company's officials, and a chaplain. There
were very few women: the wife of General Clavering, a

Miss Pearce, the wife and daughter of the Company's resident at Murshidabad, and a German lady, Mrs. Imhoff, who, with her four-year-old child, was accompanying her husband.

India was a gruelling place, for all its enticements. You had to be pretty desperate to go there, or else you had to be a very courageous man and very confident of your destiny. Many came back with riches and broken health, many with broken health only; and many came to an untimely end beneath its implacable sky. An unpleasant country, temperature one hundred degrees in January, and a shocking density of population. Seventeen thousand whites among seventy million natives. Everything was precarious, incalculable; from the moment you landed you never had firm ground under your feet. Certainly a military career there offered glamour and much more; opportunities of all kinds ran riot. Had not the thirty-year-old John Charles Maclean, brother of the Hugh Maclean on board, made forty thousand pounds in four years? Many a man would chance his liver for that.

There was no secret, then, as to what thirty-eight of the forty-one passengers on the *Duke of Grafton* were after. But what, in the name of heaven, was the German doing on the ship? This rather stout, grey-haired, gesticulating gentleman with a wife and child, who called himself Christoph Karl Adam, Baron Imhoff—though some doubt was felt about his title and the passenger list had him down as plain Mr. Imhoff. He had told some of the other passengers that he was a painter and was going to India in search of subjects and above all in the hope of painting miniatures of Indian princes on ivory and porcelain, in the mode of the day. This adventurous notion was twice as hazardous for a man who had a wife and child on his hands; his glowing enthusiasm, rendered in fluent and faulty English, was listened to with coolness. There was no response to his persistent efforts to start a conversation, and the German couple was left severely to itself.

This does not mean that the other passengers did not take a burning interest in this strange pair. Mrs. Imhoff was a great deal younger than her husband. She looked about twenty-two and she had a clear and delicate complexion, yellow hair, a beautiful skin, grey eyes, and a low forehead. She was fond of laughing, and her teeth were small and charming. Altogether, in spite of her size and height and a certain sharpness of feature at close quarters, she made a graceful and appealing impression. Whenever this dubious Baroness promenaded the deck, the manner in which the men talked and held themselves underwent a change. They talked louder and more interestingly; every gesture and movement took on a new elegance. The ladies, on the other hand, especially Mrs. Clavering, became as dumb as stones, as stiff as wood, whenever Mrs. Imhoff appeared.

There was no escape from perspiration and boredom beneath that relentless tropical sky. Three weeks on board ship is a long time, and it feels twice as long when some of the passengers form a highly sophisticated and mannered society among themselves from which you are rigidly excluded. Perhaps the German married couple suffered most from this and perhaps among all those on board they had the most dubious and difficult future before them; yet the Baron kept up his genial and ingenious efforts to make himself agreeable and the Baroness held firmly to her bright and becoming smile. She was unaffected even by the constant worry over her child. Except for the rats, this four-year-old boy was certainly the liveliest creature on the ship. With unruffled good humour his mother reproved, begged, consoled, while the little brat ran from one end of the boat to the other, playing with dog or bird, asking the Captain unintelligible questions in German, screaming, whooping, interrupting the sailors at their work, vanishing completely three or four times a week under sails or in the hold, for ever in danger of his life, crawling about and getting between people's legs. "Karl! *Karl!*" Mrs. Imhoff's ringing voice was to be heard all day long, and the passengers explained to each other that Karl meant Charles.

One day, bowling his hoop with more determination than skill, this boy Karl got in the way of Mrs. Clavering, who was pacing the deck clothed, in spite of the heat, in a splendid and voluminous dress. The hoop got caught in her train. The stout little fellow charged after it and, gripping hold of her as he fell, tore her skirt in two. The General's wife gathered her torn dress together and, with an extremely sour look on her large face, went on without a word. Mrs. Imhoff ran after her and, blushing deeply, addressed her most earnestly in a mixture of German and English, turning now and again to the boy to insist apparently on his apologizing to the lady. But the child stood, chubby-faced and stolid, staring straight in front of him with his round eyes.

The General's wife replied frigidly: "I don't understand you," and very expressively raised her shoulders and let them fall again. Then, with head high and eyes front, she walked on.

Mrs. Imhoff lost her blithe, gay look. Her back bent; her face quivered and flushed; sharp lines of pain showed around her eyes. She had suddenly become a tired, anxious woman.

Just as she turned away, holding the pouting, refractory boy by the hand, a small man in a coffee-coloured coat came up to her. He had a long face, a long nose, large eyes beneath a wide forehead, a strong chin; and his clothes, in spite of the heat, were faultlessly pressed and closely buttoned up. Speaking slowly and courteously, he said: "It must be hard making such a long journey with a child, even when the child is so charming and the mother so patient."

Mrs. Imhoff looked at the gentleman in the coffee-coloured coat and dimly remembered the Baron telling her that the little man who was so reserved was a very important person, but that no one could get near him. She smiled once more; she looked girlish and appealing. "Oh—sir," she said in broken English, "it is the opposite. It is beautiful—— It is sweet," she added, correcting herself, "to have a child with, and it is dreadful—without."

The gentleman in the coffee-coloured coat listened with attention and assured her once more very slowly and in simple words, so that she could understand him, that her boy was charming. He was probably the only person on board except the child's mother who was of this opinion. Mrs. Imhoff made an impulsive reply and begged him to excuse her terrible English. On the contrary he found her English wonderful. The Baroness was taller than he and her bright and lively manner contrasted with his gravity. The women looked on with disgust at the colloquy and the men with eager interest. The Baron came up. The three seemed to be the only ones on board whose spirits rose above the tedium and the heat. Later, they sat together at luncheon. Karl sprinkled the coffee-coloured coat with crumbs and the owner of it was delighted.

After luncheon the passengers withdrew to their cabins, and the Baron then told his spouse who and what the gentleman in the coffee-coloured coat was. He was a certain Mr. Warren Hastings. The Baroness had never before heard the name Warren and she tried hard to say it properly in her ringing Swabian speech. The Baron went on to explain that this Mr. Warren Hastings was going as second in council to Madras. And, as the governor of Madras, Mr. Du Pré, was old and no more than a figurehead, Mr. Hastings would in fact govern the Presidency. What was the Presidency of Madras? the Baroness asked with a yawn; for now she was beginning to give way blissfully to the heat and her fatigue. Was it as large as the Duchy of Württemberg? She came from Stuttgart and, until she set out on this long voyage, the only other place she had known was Nuremberg, where the Baron had been living for some years. Yes, the Presidency had a population of, maybe, twenty million; Württemberg eight hundred thousand. And so this little coffee-coloured gentleman might be considered more powerful than Duke Karl Eugen, the Baroness said, laughing in spite of herself. Yes, Karl Adam assured her seriously; and he began, not for the first time, to paint in glowing colours all the marvels of the Indian scene—that immense and teeming country with its curious, highly civilized population, so babyishly weak that any man of brains and determination could overthrow it with his little finger. Lord Clive had shown that nine hundred Englishmen were a match for fifty thousand of the natives. A funny lot, these natives. For all their cowardice they could sometimes be really dangerous; particularly where their gods and sacred animals were concerned. They gave way, bent before the storm, could not be cornered; perjured themselves time after time for a triviality and wondered that you wondered at it; died resolutely and without a word for things as trivial. Herr von Imhoff romanced about the wealth of folk-lore, the jungle, the temples, the Rajahs on thrones of gold and ivory, the holy men endowed with hypnotic powers, the temple dancing-girls, the seething masses whom any white man could make his slaves. He spoke of the immense possibilities open to any intelligent man there, now that the European constellation had risen, bringing war and the rivalries of Dutch and English and French interests. It was only necessary, perhaps, as the champion of one of the native princes, to play off the European forces one against the other. Herr von Imhoff went on to dream of how he would win the favour of one of the native potentates with his miniature painting, make himself indispensable, and then, after cutting himself a good slice out of the giant Indian cake, return laden with riches to Europe.

Marianne listened in silence, her lowered eyelids a delicate blue, fringed with long light-brown lashes. She loved her husband and loved to hear him talk; he was so romantic and adventurous. Life in Stuttgart had been tedious and restricted. She was only Anna Maria Apollonia Chapuset, third daughter of a poor French émigré family which clung to the outer edge of the pompous court of Württemberg, vainly defying a scarcely dissembled contempt. So when the Franconian Baron appeared, a much-travelled man of the world, and made ardent love to this tall and soft and inexperienced Marianne Chapuset, it is not surprising that his gallantry seemed the answer to her dreams. She made no resistance whatever and wondered that her dream could be fulfilled with such magnificent ease.

In an interview, painful from every aspect, her father and brother compelled the rather elderly and threadbare Baron to marry Marianne. Karl Adam von Imhoff had seen life, and his travels in Turkey had given him a fatalistic turn. Why not? he asked himself and married her. Her mother, Susanne Chapuset, was the only person to object. Baron Imhoff did not please her at all; a windbag, an adventurer, penniless. "This is no Selzhäfele you've got into this time," she said sadly as Marianne got into the coach with her husband. Now a Selzhäfele was a bowl of the raspberry fool which was so delicious a speciality of the country. In spite of Madame Chapuset's apprehension the marriage did not turn out so badly. They went to Nuremberg, where their first child died; this was perhaps fortunate. Later, they availed themselves, not quite irreproachably, of an opportunity of getting credit. Marianne knew nothing of business and debts did not trouble her. When matters came to a head and the Baron proposed the Indian adventure, she felt no compunction about bringing off a final *coup* on her own account and lifted a final and very considerable sum from their injured and thick-headed creditors. And now they were on the *Duke of Grafton* with a healthy child, rich in hope but short of money.

The gentleman of the coffee-coloured coat and the difficult name was also reclining on his bunk in the heat of his cabin. He had had sixteen years of India; he was used to its trying climate, its difficult situations, its gruelling experiences of every kind. He was used to making rapid decisions when the fortunes of war hung upon them and to conducting complicated diplomatic negotiations with unintelligible natives. He was used to defending measures which were as obvious in Madras or Calcutta as they were incomprehensible in the office of the East India Company in Leadenhall Street and to fighting London in London's interests. He was used to resolving the dilemma: money *or* humanity, when London wanted money *and* humanity. He was used to sampling wares, organizing transport on a huge scale, erect-

ing warehouses which were at the same time forts, dodging
the vicissitudes of wars at sea which were never far from
piracy, pulling off commercial deals in which there was a
spice of foreign policy. He enjoyed—in that intolerable
climate—jumbling up politics, strategy, native psychology,
English civilization, Indian culture, in such a fashion as to
produce a big dividend for Leadenhall Street. In his leisure
he read the Latin classics, wrote verse, went in for sport,
and learnt the languages of the country. The only thing he
winced at was having nothing to do. On board the ship
there was nothing to do but read the classics and play chess
with Major Archibald Callender. This was more than he
could endure.

He could not sleep. Lying in his hot cabin, he reflected
that with the best of luck it would be sixteen weeks before he
reached Madras. He reflected on the debts he had had to
contract in order to go on paying the generous annuities
which during his stay in England he had settled on his
numerous poor relations. He thought of Daylesford, to
which he had paid another visit—the old family property
which had been sold three generations ago. Would ten years'
labour in Madras and Bengal be too high a price to pay for

the recovery of Daylesford? He thought not—and a smile lengthened his long lips.

In the cool of the evening he encountered the German lady on deck. He really did like that boy, but he was not sorry that Baroness Imhoff had put him to bed. Mr. Hastings again wore a coffee-coloured coat, but it was a different one. The Baroness too had changed her dress: she was in a flutter of light scarves, veils, and lace; and there was a mighty erection of her blond hair. Hastings talked to her about Madras and Bengal. But not at all as Herr von Imhoff had. He spoke in figures—of tariffs and taxes and administrative measures. The Baroness listened, smiling politely, and then, glancing off these hard facts, became sentimental, as the mode enjoined. It was evident, however, that they couldn't advance far into this realm without the aid of a common language. The gentleman in brown looked attentively at her long coral lips, misunderstood if he understood at all, and both, while they lost themselves in a discussion of the influences on the soul of the tropical sky, could not help laughing often and heartily over the little either could understand of what the other said.

All the other thirty-nine passengers, also the captain and

the crew and the white and coloured servants and stewards, looked on with interest at this conversation. Mrs. Clavering remarked, first to herself and later to the others, that it was now evident in which of this married couple the taint resided. Though before she had given Mr. Imhoff the cold shoulder, she now actively took pity on a man so grossly slighted by his wife.

Mr. Hastings was used to conducting conversations in the way he wished them to go. Nothing could turn him from his goal even in those extremely tricky interviews with natives when the most crooked and flowery path was the shortest. In this conversation it was Mrs. Imhoff who took the lead. Mr. Hastings was content patiently to correct the Baroness's mistakes. She laughed. corrected herself, imprinted the correction on her memory, and the next instant made the same mistake again. Whatever she said Mr. Hastings found both sensible and enchanting.

At dinner the Baron gave the second in council at Madras his views about India. The Baron was a man of imagination, of original ideas, of unique experiences, with an eye for colour, a feeling for poetry. Mr. Hastings took to him. He delighted in poetry himself. He was employed on a translation of a short Veda. Even on his busiest days he devoted at least twenty minutes to the Muses. But he made a sharp distinction between literature and business, and his reverence for Indian and Persian poetry did not prevent him from taking a very clear view of the Company's interests when it came to dealing with Hindus and Mohammedans. As the conversation was conducted in English, Marianne was not able to follow it very well, but she threw in a banal remark here and there with arch intent.

Later, from his bunk, the Baron explained to his wife that this Mr. Hastings owed his success to the fact that he was no philosopher. The man who made long debate of the why and wherefore could never bring off a deal with real success. This Mr. Hastings would in all probability make himself undisputed master of India, precisely because he never asked himself to what end he did it. He, Karl Adam, was of course very much more gifted than this gentleman of the coffee-coloured coat. But unfortunately he was a philosopher, in a sense a poet. Therefore he had to confine himself to understanding and explaining the pie while Coffee-Colour ate it.

Marianne fell asleep very contentedly while Karl Adam was explaining this. She had a tremendous respect for her husband and his philosophy; but she did not need to be put right about the small and serious little man in the coffee-coloured coat. She liked him because she felt she was his superior. Her romantic Baron was her superior, and therefore she *loved* him.

There was a tiresome little incident the following morning. Their little boy made a mess of their cabin. The Baroness, who insisted on cleanliness, ordered the stewardess to clean it up. Scarcely had this been done when Karl repeated the offence. The girl, when summoned again, made a face. The Baroness asked Karl Adam to give the person a tip. Karl Adam declared that it was quite beyond his power. Though he was not wedded to money for money's sake, the fifteen louis-d'or he still possessed were earmarked for their stay in India. They would last at longest a week, and he had made a stern resolve not to break into them. The girl stood there during this discussion without stirring a finger. She certainly did not understand the German, but she no doubt understood its meaning. When nothing came of it, she left the cabin without having carried out the Baroness's order. Marianne wondered whether to make a complaint and decided that it would be better to beg the girl to do what she asked after mollifying her with the gift of a small brooch.

The Baron now dressed for dinner with unusual magnificence—with much greater magnificence than the second member of the Madras Council, who continued as before to ring the changes on his two coffee-coloured coats. But Imhoff's satin coat was a little the worse for wear and his peruke was in need of renovation; and the contrast between him and the severe Mr. Hastings was by no means to his advantage. Marianne was voluble in German; when she spoke in English she made the same mistakes as she had the first day. She observed that the correct Mr. Hastings found her Swabian prattle just as entrancing as her faulty English. She loved her husband and decided to be Mrs. Hastings.

Mrs. Clavering now spent a great deal of time with Baron Imhoff. If Marianne joined them, Mrs. Clavering became as wood; she did not open her mouth and quickly excused herself. Marianne decided to become Mrs. Hastings and to take precedence of the General's wife.

Three days later Warren Hastings fell sick. The Reverend A. Salmon, though he had studied medicine, could not diagnose the disorder. He prescribed—as a shot in the air—a febrifuge. But what his patient was suffering from was having nothing to do; for he never felt well except under pressure of incessant work.

Marianne Imhoff sat in his hot and ill-ventilated cabin

nursing his illness. She gazed at his long nose, which projected abruptly from his forehead and seemed twice as long as ever on his emaciated face. She gazed at his strong chin, his commanding forehead, whose lofty expanse was the higher because at thirty-seven his hair was beginning to recede. She hung on every word that issued from his thin, dry lips, and understood nearly all he said. She understood that he talked of power, of military operations, and knew that here and there he quoted Latin. She had often heard Latin in Stuttgart and could not help laughing at the English pronunciation—and the sick man, who clearly did not know she was there, laughed too.

This proved to Marianne Imhoff, who loved her husband Karl Adam, that she and this man Hastings with the difficult first name could live happily together, and she made up her mind, come what might, to nurse him back to health. In spite of the scandal she never left his cabin day or night from that day on.

As soon as Hastings began to recover and was for the first time clear in his mind, he asked for a looking-glass. He had often been in danger of his life; he had mastered desperate situations without a tremor; the admonition of Horace—to keep a cool head in hard straits—was his device. But when he saw his unkempt and bearded face in the glass, he visibly quailed and, losing for once all control of his nerves, demanded the barber. Marianne did not understand what he said, but she guessed his meaning. With the swiftness of instinct she found his razor, made a lather, and prepared to shave him. He protested in alarm; for it was highly improper. But Marianne insisted and, after three-quarters of an hour, without inflicting more than five serious gashes, she restored his face to its former state.

Warren Hastings was aware during this proceeding of a deep and intimate sympathy, improper but exceedingly welcome, between this woman and himself. He resolved, with a determination equal to that of his resolve to complete and maintain the conquest of India, to have the marriage between her and Baron Imhoff, whom he liked very well, dissolved, and to make her Mrs. Hastings.

As soon as he was able to go on deck, he asked the Baron to paint a miniature of him. The other passengers thought it a little odd of the second in council at Madras to have his portrait painted by this obscure German. He sat first in his coffee-coloured coat and then in his wine-red frock coat.

There was no denying, all the same, that despite his small stature he looked very imperious in his wine-red coat and large peruke, with his great forehead and the long nose jutting straight out from it, and his heavy eyebrows and forceful chin. Even the boy Karl was a good deal impressed.

During the sittings Mr. Hastings talked to Mr. Imhoff about German, English, and Indian Law, with particular reference to marriage. Mr. Hastings had won political, military, and commercial victories; but he had never been so pleased as when he learnt that in the Franconian courts a divorce could be obtained on the ground of mutual dislike, or incompatibility of temperament.

Warren Hastings was now very quickly restored to health, for he had something to do. He stalked the fanciful, corpulent Baron with the patience he had learnt in the long-drawn-out negotiations of the East. The Baron saw him coming and knew that the battle was lost before it was even begun. He loved Marianne and he was impressed by Hastings. They both had more energy than he. He had too much imagination to be energetic; he saw too many roads to be able to keep to one. Pleasant though his marriage was, he was ready as a fatalist to shrug his shoulders and slip out of it just as he had slipped into it. Also—as a fatalist he did not shut his eyes to this side of the question—there were advantages. A clever man might help himself out of the open hand of this young Indian conqueror. Herr von Imhoff, busy with his India ink and his brush, drove a hard bargain. There were long and flowery preludes before the two were able to lay their cards on the table without disguise. Then it was found that their views were really not diametrically opposed. Mr. Hastings was as generous in the matter of money as Mr. Imhoff in affairs of the feelings.

That very night the Baron came to an understanding with Marianne. At first he tried to be worldly, sceptical, cynical; but it did not come off very well. His plump face looked weary and old and Marianne loved him dearly. She tried to make a farce of the whole affair, and her little teeth gleamed as she laughed and laughed. But this attempt failed too. Finally she cried. It was only the second time during all the years they had lived together that Karl Adam had seen her cry; for she was an exception in that age of feeling and was not fond of tears. This time she cried until the whole pillow was wet. She tried to stifle her sobs in it, but the child woke up and became difficult and demanded lemonade and made a noise and there were complaints from the cabins on either side.

It was next decided that the Imhoffs should send their petition for divorce to the courts of law at Nuremberg from the next port the boat put in at, and then remain in Madras, or wherever else Mr. Hastings might be, until the German decree arrived. Mr. Hastings undertook to provide for their maintenance in a manner suitable to their rank, since under this new dispensation Mr. Imhoff was no longer able to pursue his original scheme of making a fortune from his miniatures. When the divorce was accomplished, Mr. Imhoff was to return to Germany and Karl to remain with his mother.

Once all this had been arranged, the Imhoffs and Karl and Mr. Warren Hastings led a united family life for the remainder of the voyage. Herr von Imhoff was reconciled to his destiny. The other thirty-eight passengers were scarcely of the same way of thinking. Least of all Mrs. Clavering. She behaved as frigidly to Mr. Imhoff and Mr. Hastings as she had before to Mrs. Imhoff only.

II

It took six years, however, before the legal formalities were concluded. In those years Warren Hastings became Governor of Bengal and first Governor-General of British

India. He completed the conquest of India. He filled the Company's coffers. He broke the malicious and pig-headed opposition of those members of the council who had been sent from London to tie his hands. To this end he had an Indian Rajah hanged. For the same purpose he destroyed a brave race which he admired, to please a cowardly one which disgusted him. He made roads. Relieved famines. Was just and unjust, even as the river Ganges.

Marianne Imhoff was at his side and understood not a thing of all that went on. She kept house in Calcutta like a princess, dressed with elegance and luxury, spent lacs of rupees, allowed the princes and great personages of the country to make her presents which they wrathfully and with extreme devotion laid at her feet, laughed and made the most of her small teeth, felt herself the superior of Warren Hastings and liked him very much, spoke bad English and did nothing to improve it; and Hastings found everything about her wonderful. Her long neck grew scraggy, her features sharp, and her boy Karl became a lanky, noisy, unpleasant lout.

Just as Warren Hastings had by a series of bold and high-handed strokes broken the opposition of the three hostile members of the council, the decree of divorce arrived from the courts of Nuremberg, and he was able to make Mrs. Imhoff an honest woman. General Clavering was one of the three councillors whom he had defeated; and in view of the truce which had only just been patched up the General could scarcely refuse to attend the wedding. Two days before the ceremony the General conveniently fell sick. His wife excused herself on the ground that she had to nurse her husband. But Hastings, at Marianne's wish, made a personal call on the General on the day of the wedding and politely but obstinately insisted that he and Lady Clavering should take part in the festivities.

Marianne's life had been almost uniformly happy. She was happy at Stuttgart when she lost her heart to the Baron; she was happy when she married him; she was happy when she put the baby Karl for the first time to her breast; she was happy when on board the boat the heart beneath the coffee-coloured coat warmed towards her. But the happiest day of her life was when she received the congratulations of the General's wooden wife.

General Clavering died three days after the Governor's wedding, possibly from overwork, possibly from the rancour that devoured his heart.

III

Marianne wrote to her mother, Susanne Chapuset, to tell her of her new marriage and enclosed a large cheque. The letter went from Calcutta to Plymouth and reached her mother's hands eighteen weeks after it was written. The self-important old lady was inclined to agree with the court circle of Stuttgart in looking down with disdain on the Governor of India. India—a sort of menagerie, a circus; its Governor—something between a shopkeeper and a tamer of wild beasts. That kind of thing did not go down at Stuttgart. When, ten months after the dispatch of her letter, Marianne received her mother's answer, she read cordial wishes for her happiness, but also the sad comment that Marianne had not this time, either, put herself in the Selzhäfele. Now by Selzhäfele she meant those bowls of raspberry fool which were so delicious a speciality of Württemberg.

IV

Mr. Warren Hastings, seventy-two years of age, wearing, in defiance of the fashion, a plain coffee-coloured coat, was walking alone through the carefully tended gardens at Daylesford. It was a June morning and still very early. Daylesford House, white and peaceful and stately, looked across the wide park over a pretty lake. The servants were only just astir. The old gentleman observed with pleasure how well certain shrubs he had introduced from Bengal were coming on, though others—the lychee trees, for example, which he had with great trouble got from Madras—he was sorry to see were not likely to bear fruit here. He bent down to read the botanical name written neatly on a label attached to one of the trees: Nephelium litchi.

The sun rose slowly above the trees. He went into the breakfast room. Three places were laid. His eye was caught by a squat bowl of grey earthenware of a sort not made in England. He smiled. The bowl was doubtless for the guest who had arrived the day before.

And here she came—a very old lady; Marianne led her in and Hastings kissed her with immense reverence. It was Marianne's mother.

Yes, old Susanne Chapuset had at last arrived from Stuttgart. She had not seen her daughter since she left with Karl Adam that day for Nuremberg. Madame Chapuset had heard many marvels, certainly, about Marianne's career and had also from time to time received many solid tokens of her existence in the form of cheques and hard cash. Nevertheless, she had not overcome her sceptical attitude towards that uncouth foreign land where Marianne lived, nor allowed herself to be bluffed by anything so equivocal as a Governor of India. It was only since her daughter became the mistress of Daylesford that she began to admit that the marriage with Mr. Hastings might not have been a *mésalliance* after all. So now, after thirty-five years, at the age of seventy-seven, she had set off to have a look at her rascal of a son-in-law.

Marianne, meanwhile, had lived in India like a queen. She gave the Governor-General many a tight corner to get out of owing to things she said or did which he himself thought charming—and had to apologize for if the worst came to the worst by pleading her defective English. Then for the sake of her health she left India before her husband and came to London, where she found many a Mrs. Clavering ready to look askance at her as a *divorcée* of questionable repute, and gave herself up with passion to the task of correcting their obliquity of vision for them. This occupied her so exclusively that, when the Governor-General on his return to England was impeached before Parliament for his conduct in India, she scarcely noticed this mammoth trial.

She had spent a great deal of money and generously come to the help of her numerous uncles, aunts, nephews, nieces, cousins of both sexes, and, of course, her former husband, Baron Imhoff, who now, married once more, was roving round Germany and Austria. She had put her son Charles— a fat, red, boorish fellow—into a very fine job. And now at Daylesford she spoke the same broken English as she had on the *Duke of Grafton* and made the same mistakes, which Mr. Hastings was just as happy as ever to correct.

Marianne led her mother to the breakfast table. The old lady looked out with pleasure at the lake and garden. Then she sat down and comfortably surveyed the breakfast table —but started at the sight of that unwieldy earthenware dish. For a moment she was puzzled, and then broke out into a hearty laugh. It was a bowl of raspberry fool, a real genuine Selzhäfele from Württemberg.

So there they were, the three of them, Hastings drinking tea, Marianne and the old lady coffee. The two ladies smiled as they put their hands out for the Selzhäfele and smiled as they helped themselves. It had cost Marianne no end of bother to get it from Stuttgart; but of this she said nothing. It was not necessary. But there was a great deal else the two ladies gossiped about in their nimble Swabian speech.

Sir Warren found the dear, respected mother of his wife wonderful. It was a pity, though, that he could not understand a single word she said; for she spoke only German and this was one of the few languages he did not know. Nevertheless, he listened now and then, smiling politely and happily.

Mother Chapuset stayed only four days. Sir Warren put her on board the boat and saw that she had every possible attention. He was respectful and assiduous—it was a pity only that he could not exchange one word with her. He stood for a long time looking after the ship. On his return he called in at East India House, in order to keep his eye on an affair of importance. But he made the interview as brief as possible, for he longed to be back at Daylesford and to hear the voice of his wife.

ALTITUDE
RECORD

ALTITUDE RECORD

On July 2nd, a very hot day, Lieutenant Victor Crécy took off at 10.20 a.m. to break the world altitude record of 11,454 metres.

The highest limit attainable by an aeroplane was mathematically ascertainable. There was not, however, in spite of many laboratory experiments, any formula that could establish with certainty the height to which a human being could ascend and live. Five airmen had so far made systematic and determined attempts to beat the record. Lieutenant Crécy was the sixth.

His machine. *Marie Lemaire (S A III 26)*, climbed in circles up into the thin, wind-swept atmosphere. For from the edge of airless space a strong east wind unceasingly whipped past. The horizon rose with the machine, *Marie Lemaire,* and grew more distant and less distinct. Lieutenant Crécy kept gaining height, slowly, carefully, knowing well that the human body, if it was suddenly taken to such heights, would burst; for the vacancy of space sucks at every inch of the body, greedy for the modicum of air it contains, and draws the blood out through the skin.

In a short time, slow as the ascent seemed, the lieutenant reached the icy regions of extreme height. A few clouds, a snowstorm that came from nowhere and would never reach the earth . . . on he soared alone.

The levers of his 280 h.p. engine danced; now and again the blades of his propeller were visible. Beyond this the flyer saw nothing but the delicate pointers of his instruments. Long since, towns had shrunk to hand's-breadths and then vanished, and the rivers had shrunk to thin threads and vanished too. There was no sound but the throb of the engine. Space held nothing but him and his machine.

Lieutenant Crécy was twenty-eight years old; he had been twice mentioned in French dispatches for exceptional services. Now he had set himself the task of laying before the International Aeronautical Federation in Paris sealed instruments with readings and results which the Federation could set up as the record. Eleven altitude flights as well as experiments in the laboratory had acquainted him with the effects of a rarefied atmosphere. He knew how the white midsummer sun blazed with relentless intensity when the atmosphere afforded no protection. He knew well the freezing wintry cold of these altitudes even in July. Crécy was closely wrapped in furs and wore heavy fur gloves; besides this, one of his legs, which was permanently stiff and therefore quickly sensitive to cold, was warmed by an electric radiator. His face was thickly smeared with grease. His eyes, in one of which was stuck a monocle, were protected by large goggles.

He climbed higher. In spite of all precautions the wind cut into his bones like a saw. His face was blistered in spite of the grease. The metal parts of the machine contracted in the cold and pieces broke off like brittle slate because of the vibration of the engine. He breathed in oxygen through a little tube, as if he were smoking a pipe.

Lieutenant Victor Crécy, at a height of between 9000 and 9500 metres, rejoiced in the thought that no other living being had ever climbed into just this part of space. He was a brave man. He had behind him battles with dreaded foes; he had crashed from a great—it had seemed an endless—height, spitting bullets as he fell, and there he had lain among the trenches and the wire. His keen, impassive face—a poker face, his friends called it—with his machine, *Marie Lemaire*, as foil, was the joy of photographers and known to millions of men as the indisputable emblem of the intrepidity of their generation.

But suddenly at 10 300 metres, this face became contorted beneath the thick layer of grease and the mouth helplessly gaped and shut again. The lieutenant no longer heard the engine; the view became indistinct; tongue and throat went dry; he was prostrated with hunger. It grew darker; soon it would be night. He began talking to himself—a thing he had never done. "10,734 metres under the sea . . . my mother is not really black, brown rather. I've been climbing for 2900 hours and only just 11 metres up. I'd like a beefsteak now. Damnable how the time passes. I read 29, but it's 92 actually."

Just as he was losing consciousness and the sun began to melt away into bights and promontories and to waggle about very curiously, he noticed that the oxygen in the frozen automatic apparatus had given out. Mechanically he seized the reserve bottle. All other thoughts were swept away in the fraction of a second by the urgent command: the controls—the controls!

The sun recovered its brilliance: the engine roared in the same rhythm as before. His hunger was gone. He knew that his mother was fair and that he had taken off at 10.20, and so had not yet been seventy minutes in the air. At that

Lieutenant Crécy laughed aloud, a burst of youthful ringing laughter; but at that height in space it did not ring out very far. He looked at the altimeter and saw he had reached 11,156 metres.

He accomplished the next 100 metres slowly and surely —as though he had only been 4000 metres up. But then the machine began to rock; it flew arbitrarily in the thin air without obeying the rudder. Colder than the cold of empty space was the thought that his oxygen would not hold out till he out-distanced the 11,454 metres which John Macready had achieved. Time crept slowly and leadenly on. Again he began gasping, felt his heart beating, fought for breath. He forced himself to think of the laboratory experiments and to believe that this was only an early phase and without danger. But so many fishes flocked towards him, big and little, glassy-eyed and stupid, defying the alien element. He knew in flashes that he was flying at a very great height, and also that something was wrong. He knew that it could be corrected by a simple grip of his hand. He gasped painfully for breath, but could not make his hand grip. It was all these fishes flocking round that prevented him.

Now he got to it. He must do something with the middle lever. He lifted his hand. Then the lever rushed away from it, it eluded his grasp, now to the front, now to the left; he could not find that damned lever. He raised his large goggles, presumably to clear away the flocks of fishes, and bared his eyes—in the left one his monocle was stuck. He felt a stab to his brain and then nothing more.

The machine, *Marie Lemaire (S A III 26)*, was picked up the same day, floating on the water. Oddly enough it was not very greatly damaged. The dead lieutenant sat in the cockpit, his hand frozen to the joystick; his eyes, too, were frozen, and the monocle was still stuck in the left one. The sealed instruments showed that he had reached a height of 11,901 metres, 447 metres higher than the record.

BULLFIGHT

BULLFIGHT

The arena—cheap places in the sun, dear ones in the shade—had been sold out for nearly a week; people had come in from all over the province to see the procession in the morning, the bullfight in the late afternoon. For the programme of this *corrida,* which by the way had been got up for the benefit of an international humanitarian organization, the Red Cross, announced the bullfighter Montilla II, who had won his way to the first rank, an *espada* of the highest distinction—after the dictator, the most talked-of man in Spain.

The painter, Greiderer, although he had only a smattering of Spanish, made excited and affable attempts to talk to his neighbour, who replied with animation. Without either understanding very much of what the other said, the Bavarian and the Spaniard kept up a lively conversation with many gesticulations and much pleasure in the interest they mutually aroused. To the painter Greiderer, who was very susceptible to any kind of show or pageantry that had its roots in the people, this bullfight was the high-water mark of his Spanish tour. He had heard a great deal about the gore and the disembowelled horses and such-like gruesome details; he waited in eager suspense.

The procession of the morning had made a great impression on him. An impassioned connoisseur, whose taste had been formed by the Munich Corpus Christi processions, he had not let a detail escape him. In endless succession had passed before him the rich and brilliant vestments of the priests, the effigies of saints shimmering in barbaric splendour on platforms borne along by many unseen men whose dull rhythmic tread evoked a feeling of weird excitement, the garish uniforms of officers and officials, the church banners, the endless treasures of the cathedral, the tramp of marching soldiers. Horses, men, and guns. And all the way over flowers thickly strewn on the ground, beneath awnings that crossed the street to ward off the glare of the sun, between carpets hung from every window and balcony. At all this the painter Greiderer had looked on.

Now in the afternoon all the thousands who had walked in the procession sat in the amphitheatre, filling the stone tiers right up to the blinding sky, letting their brilliant scarves trail from seat to seat, waiting, after the incense, the martyred saints, and holy pageantry of the morning, for the blood of the bulls, the eviscerated horses, the tossed and trampled men. Sellers of beer, sweets, fruit, programmes, fans, cried their wares. Advertisement sheets littered every row of seats. Enormous grey conical felt hats of the men, showy scarves of the women. Outcry, suspense, sweat, excitement.

But now the *cuadrilla* entered the arena, marching in quick step to lively music, in brightly coloured, elaborately embroidered jackets. Rapidly they scattered over the clean expanse of sand. In a moment the bull came in—stopping dead, after long hours in the dark, at the sight of the jubilant throng in the fierce light. He charged the red cloths that gave way before him. Next there were the horses, wretched nags with their eyes bandaged, ridden by men with lances, their feet in enormous stirrups. The bull, black, massive, with lowered head, lifted one sorry beast on his horns and with surprising slowness tossed horse and rider behind him. This happened immediately in front of Greiderer, who was sitting near the front and low down. He saw the coarse face of the costumed picador. There was a grinding, cracking noise as the bull plunged his horns into the horse; Greiderer saw him turn his horns about in the beast's bowels, wrench his horns out of its belly, drenched in blood and entrails; then in again, out again. Herrgott-sakra!—but that was something very different from the babble of a fellow-artist he had listened to about a series of tiles called "The Bullfight." The excitement which swept over the thirteen thousand other spectators caught the Bavarian painter, Andreas Greiderer, too, and shook him.

The bull, provoked by the cloths of the fellows in gay costume, turned upon another horse that had meanwhile been brought into the arena. Its rider pricked out a piece of flesh and black hide with his lance. The bull threw the horse down. Trembling, covered with blood and dirt, it was pulled to its feet again and with great difficulty ridden again at the bull. This time it was caught on the horns and gored. The rider limped off. The horse groaned, neighed, tried again and again to rise to its feet, until a man in a red jacket finished it off.

Fellows with short darts decorated with coloured frills now take up their positions in front of the bull. Each stands alone, elegant, provoking him with shouts of mockery. They run up to within a foot or two of his snorting nostrils, stepping aside at the last moment to plunge the decorated javelins into his flesh and leave them sticking there. The crowd follows every movement, greeting it, according to the art displayed, with a roar of applause or howls of disgust. The bull, stuck about with the tormenting coloured darts and trickling with streams of blood, runs about the arena, faced now by one, now by another. One he knocks over and wounds, but not fatally.

Now a man walks alone to the front of the Prefect's box and takes off his two-cornered hat. This is the matador. It is not Montilla II. But all the same an *espada* of rank and fame, and highly paid. He faces the bull. In his left hand he holds the red cloth, in his right the sword. Advancing close up to the bull he plays him with the red cloth, on tiptoe, with feet together, lightly balanced, coolheaded, motionless except for the upper half of his body, which sways to one side so that the bull charges empty space and rushes past. Then back again. He plays the raging beast as if it were a marionette on a wire, risking death as the penalty for the slightest error of movement. Every turn of his body is greeted by the thirteen thousand with a yell of applause, and since they follow closely on one another as the bull passes to and fro, the great amphitheatre is shattered by short rhythmic bursts of applause.

But now it was the last time. The *espada* stood with his

sword pointed along his cheek, aiming as he faced the bull, small, elegant, shoulders braced. But either through bad luck or a blunder in his technique the sword did not reach the heart; the beast shook it aside. The infuriated crowd whistled.

The painter Greiderer did not understand why the public was jubilant nor why it was enraged; his neighbour endeavoured to explain how the bull, according to the rules, ought to be dispatched. Greiderer was not much the wiser, but he went with the crowd. He trembled with the same excitement as ran through the shouting, whistling, jubilating throng. When his neighbour and countless others threw down their hats at the feet of the *espada,* who, after finally killing the bull according to the rules of the art, headed the triumphal procession, the painter Greiderer of Munich also flung his expensive and recently purchased Spanish hat with all his force into the arena.

The fourth bull was whistled out of the ring. He showed himself a coward. This animal, when his end drew near, was so mean-spirited as to wish to die in peace. He ignored the provocative red cloths, he was deaf to shouts of scorn. He had been reared near Cordova on a flat plain deep in rich cool grass, beneath a wide sky, the resort of many storks.

BULLFIGHT

He had grown to his full size, to a weight of 900 libras. Now he stood there surrounded by these thousands, stuck about with coloured darts, dripping with blood, moaning dully in his pain, making water, longing for death. Pressed up against the palisade he took no heed of the human herd; even fire and gunpowder thrust between his legs roused the beast no more. He wanted no more of the sand and the sun. He wanted to stay where he was up against the palisade in the shadow and die.

The painter Greiderer looked on, sunk in himself, his sly, furrowed peasant's face pale with passionate concern. He did not grasp what was going on—why the people roared, now for the bull, now for the bullfighter. He had seen many people die, in bed, in battle, in the Munich street-fighting, in brawls. But this play of blood and sand and sun, this carefully regulated, purposeless duel, this magnificent and abhorrent drama—in which the death, cruel and very real, of pitiable horses, of infuriated beasts, and perhaps, too, of one of those elegant duellists, was made the sport of spectators—shook his drama-loving soul more than any other death he had ever seen.

When it was over, he drove through the crowded evening streets to his hotel. The children were playing at bullfights. One was the bull and charged with lowered head another who waved a cloth. But the bull did not approve of the bullfighter's posture and beat him soundly. The painter Greiderer, hunched up in a corner of the car, was lost in gloom. "Swine—pudding face!" he muttered, thinking of his friend's artistic tiles called "The Bullfight." From that day on the picture of the real bull, pressed up against the palisade, making water, caring no more for men, swords, garish cloths, eager only to die in the shade, was deeply bitten into the surface of his mind.

POLAR
EXPEDITION

POLAR EXPEDITION

When he was fourteen, the Northerner read of the privations of the polar explorer Sir John Franklin and his companions; how for weeks they lived on bones they found in a deserted Indian camp till at last they devoured their own leather boots. The ambition to overcome similar hardships flamed up in him as he read. He was a taciturn boy. Without telling anyone what was in his mind he began on a fantastic course of training, driving muscle and nerve to their utmost. Near the town where he lived there was a plateau never yet traversed during winter by any living being. At the age of twenty-one he crossed it in January, saved from starvation only by an extreme power of endurance, after being frozen fast one night in a snow hole which froze to solid ice while he slept the sleep of utter exhaustion.

Tough and methodical, he learnt all that a polar explorer could need to know—the science of the sea and the sky. When he had passed his examinations, he chose for his voyages the oceans where hardships were greatest in order to learn from practical experience all the arts, big and little, of navigation and ice travel. He became a hard and silent man during months of hunger, frost, and scurvy, and stored his knowledge and experience in his brain, banking them there distrustfully and taking no pleasure in his fellow-men, believing no man but himself.

He extorted the means for his first independent expedition; for he was without scruple in money matters. He crossed the polar seas in a course never before completed. He forced the north-west passage after three years of labour, an enterprise in which all before him had come to grief. All the world acclaimed the achievement. He himself the loudest. He was indefatigable in trumpeting his exploits, carefully weighing and reckoning up the measure of his success and how far it exceeded that of any of his predecessors or rivals.

Encouraged by his success he set out for the North Pole. Another was before him. Wasting no time he turned about and made for the South Pole. On this quest, too, another had the start of him. A grim race began. The Northerner, with cold calculation, pitted against the other the accumulated experience so carefully filed in his brain. Could he spy out a mistake in his rival's preparations that he could avoid himself? He found such a mistake, the mistake. The other man had taken ponies with him; he himself banked on the hardiness and the flesh of his dogs, which are both transport and food. The other, with his ponies, met disaster; he himself returned victorious. He paid his competitor, now defeated and dead, the tribute of his admiration. But he did not forget to tell the world very clearly that the man owed his failure and his death to the mistake of relying on ponies. If he himself had triumphed, it was due to the inspiration of taking dogs. He owed it not to his luck but to his merit.

Soon afterwards he had the great idea of his life, to reach the Pole by a new and better method, by airship. The prosecution of the idea and the effort to make sure of an airship for his next polar expedition brought him into touch with the Southerner. The Northerner had been made even harder and more overbearing by success—morose and given to villainous ill-humour. His face was as gnarled as a hundred-year-old olive tree, his mouth was twisted. He was not a lovable man; his own mother could not say that of him. There were few he did not hold in contempt and many he hated with an icy ferocity. There was no one he loved. From all he exacted unquestioning submission to his authority. The Southerner, with whom he had now to work, was his exact opposite: lovable, adroit, superficial, boyishly optimistic, childishly vain in success, in misfortune overwhelmed by despair. The vivacious, charming Southerner and the stubborn, morose Northerner sniffed at each other. Neither liked the other's smell. Both had unbounded ambition; both were domineering and unscrupulous. There were clashes as soon as negotiations began, but there was only one way to the Pole and it led through the Northerner, and there was only one airship capable of the expedition and the Southerner who built it was its master. The Southerner had constructed the airship and was a good pilot. The Northerner had completed the north-west passage and knew the Arctic and the Antarctic. It is a risk when a man who has never put on skis trusts himself to another for a journey over the limitless ice. It is a risk when a man who has never flown trusts himself to another's leadership for a flight into unknown desolation, where the slightest error spells death. An equal necessity, an identical goal linked these opposites together. Neither was willing to share the success. Each hoped to jockey the other out of his share of it while they were on the way to attain it.

POLAR EXPEDITION

And, behold, the airship reached its goal. It flew over the Pole.

Whose was the success?

The Northerner had had the idea, had planned their course and prepared for it. Behind him were thirty years of indefatigable, methodical polar exploration. All that the other had known of the Pole six months earlier was that it was cold there. And now this hanger-on demanded a share, in fact the greater share, of the glory.

The Northerner growled; he called the other an irresponsible, effeminate dandy, obsessed by childish megalomania. The world heard what the Northerner had to say, allowed its truth, and unwillingly paid him its tribute of admiration. But left it at that. No support was forthcoming to enable him to proceed to further exploits. No doubt, he put difficulties in the way. He was scientific to the point of pedantry. It was his principle to foresee every situation that might possibly arise and to eliminate chance. This was not cheap. It was very expensive. As always, they grudgingly allowed the morose and overbearing man his fame, but not the means of equipping a fresh expedition.

The Southerner had better fortune. He laughed at the Northerner for a gloomy, intolerant, and pathological egoist. Imagine him wanting to take all the credit for the exploit! It was merely laughable. Any child could see that flying over the Pole was the pilot's achievement and all the Northerner knew of an airship engine was that it made a noise. People conceded the Southerner his amusement. He had the sympathy of the whole world; there was such a glamour about him.

He had the knack of shining in any situation. To keep down the weight he had compelled the Northerner to leave his furs behind. But he had secretly included his own uniform as an officer in the army of his country. When they reached the limit of the Arctic Zone on their return and the members of the expedition, soberly clad in their working kit, stepped from the ship which took them back to civilization, he appeared suddenly in his brilliant uniform. Crowds were waiting, and the little girl gave her bouquet not to the sulky Northerner in his black workman's clothes but to the gorgeous officer.

It was not she only—every heart in his whole quickly kindled country flew to him. His career was made; though still a young man he was a general. When he planned another flight over the Pole, his country at once built him an airship to his own specifications—25 metres high, 115 metres long, 1900 cubic metres capacity, four gondolas. The tanks held fuel for 75 hours, the engines were 720 horse-power. Apart from all this, the Southerner was not very thorough in his preparations. He made no great study of the science of snow and ice and Arctic conditions. Had he not got the most perfect vehicle that ever set out for the Pole, a picked crew, the most up-to-date apparatus? He trusted to his luck for the rest.

He was *fêted* and honoured, bells pealed, bands played. His ship took to the air and reached the north in three stages. Then it started on the last crucial hop. The listening world heard by wireless that he was on the way to the Pole—that he was now over Greenland and now beyond it. In twenty minutes he would be at the Pole.

Now he was over the Pole. For two hours, swelling with triumph, he circled round the white and so long coveted wilderness. The gramophone played his country's national anthem. His country's flag and a large cross blessed by the Pope were let down to the earth. He informed his King, the Pope, and the Dictator of his country that with God's help he had reached the Pole. Long live the Fatherland!

The Northerner sat in a well-equipped wireless station in the town where he lived; his eyes were stonier than usual and his twisted mouth even more grimly set. As audience he lived through each moment as his rival, the contemptible, the incompetent, reached the Pole and circled round it. He himself had devoted endless years of unflinching toil to that aim, endless nights of mortal peril. Now his exploits were worthless, his fame wiped out. This other accomplished with ease, almost without preparation, with the smile and the bow of a performer, what he had staked a lifetime to attain.

Ah, if only the ship had been his! What attention, what judgment and accuracy would have gone to the equipment of it. That fellow, his rival, was haphazard, even as a pilot. He had seen it, he knew it with the unerring insight of hate. The expedition had been frivolously undertaken—a criminal frivolity to be above that ice without exact knowledge of its nature. But this rival had luck on his side; and a face the world found pleasing. He had that lovely ship, those lovely engines, all the lovely instruments. The Northerner had the capacity; the other had the airship and the luck.

He sat at the wireless station and listened to it all. He was man enough to play audience to the other's good luck to the bitter end. The other's wireless told of his return

flight. Not a hitch of course. All well on board. Mist—
yes. More mist—a very great deal of mist. No doubt he
put it on a bit. Head wind, visibility bad. Ah, well, you
can't expect everything, my friend. But you have your
frivolity, your happy-go-lucky blindness, and—your luck.
You'll soon be safe on firm land. I hear it all; I'm waiting
here for your return. He sat on and waited; he was going
to drink the wormwood to the dregs.

But what's this? Difficulties mount up. The rudder is
not working as it should. The ship is drifting in the mist.
One of the engines has failed. The operator still announced:
all well on board. Then he announced nothing more.

The Northerner had sat since the early evening in the
wireless station. It was now nearly morning and the staff
had been relieved three times. He was stiff with his vigil,
but felt no hunger; he sat on and on waiting to hear that
the other man was safely back.

Midday came. No news. Perhaps he was drifting in the
mist; perhaps a forced landing; perhaps his wireless apparatus had given out. The hours passed and there seemed
no likelihood that he would return that day. The Northerner stood up, bent and stiff from sitting crouched so long,
and went home.

Next day the air was still dumb. The Southerner carried fuel for 75 hours. Fifty hours had gone, sixty, seventy-five. The ship was overdue.

Days went by, nights went by. The Southerner was still missing. The Northerner was now the only living man who had led an expedition by airship over the Arctic seas.

Days went by, nights went by. Then over the air came a message from the Southerner. His ship had exploded; he, with some of his crew, was on an ice-floe 180 kilometres from North Cape.

The whole world was in a fever. Was there a chance of rescuing the man? How long could he hold out? Would the ice break up? Had he food? Was he adrift? Ships were sent out—aeroplanes.

The Northerner's countrymen looked to him. The world looked to him. His government called upon him to go to the help of the shipwrecked man. Who, if not he, could rescue those derelict men?

He was accustomed to minute preparations, accustomed to seize the favourable moment after long calculation. He had his prudence, not his luck, to thank for all he had hitherto achieved. Now he was to start overnight with a machine brought to him at a moment's notice and hastily converted to serve his purpose. But then—he was the one man: his fame enjoined it on him. Also it would be a grim triumph to rescue the castaway, who fancied himself his equal, his superior, in his aeroplane. He agreed to go. The pressmen photographed him as he climbed into the machine, his lips tight, his eyes as hard as ever.

It was the last time he was photographed. He did not rescue the other man in his aeroplane. He never returned.

The man to return was the other. He had had a hard time of it—adrift on an ice-floe, with a broken leg, with death in sight, among men who saw in him the cause of their disaster. The only one of them all who had had experience of Arctic expeditions was dead. He had gone off across the ice with two others to reach firm land. He had been frozen to death on the way, or had died of hunger, or been eaten by his companions. Nobody knew.

But what everybody now knew was that the Southerner had been rescued before his men: he, their captain, before the others; that he was the cause of the Northerner's death and the deaths of eight more; and that the survivors owed their rescue to the ice-breaker of a country which in every cultural and political aspect was the bitterest enemy of his.

He was the man who first traversed the Arctic sky in

machines he himself designed and built and flew. Only a few weeks before the world had paid him homage far above his desert, far above any tribute ever paid the Northerner. Now it spat on him. Now he was a coward, a smirch on his country's honour, a mockery, an exasperation.

The other was dead—dead because of him and for his sake. He lived—the only living being to fly an airship over the Pole. But the other was the great man; while he was a laughing-stock, whom even his country disowned.

THE
LITTLE
SEASON

THE LITTLE SEASON

The little old gentleman whose severe expression and locks of white hair suggested the actor or the cleric was walking along the lakeside promenade at Vörtschau. As he went by with one hand behind his back, wearing a well-preserved but old-fashioned and rather too long coat, a white tie, and a wide-brimmed, pinched-in felt hat, he had the air of someone of importance who was accustomed to being taken notice of. Also he was by no means close-fisted and did not look twice at a ten-shilling note. And yet the inhabitants made heavy and not at all amiable fun of him when he had passed. It had been a poor season, and one old boy does not make a summer. Poor Austria, unlike the German Empire, had stabilized her currency; hence living was dear for Germans at Vörtschau, their beloved Carinthian summer resort; and the place, though it relied on German summer visitors, had seen remarkably few of them. Moreover it had rained. The season was over before its time. The Hotel Mangart had dismissed most of its staff already and closed the main building. Meals were served in the annex. The café and *pâtisserie* were closed. The bathing-establishment was still at the disposal of visitors, though there was no staff there and they had to look after themselves. The branches of Vienna firms had put up their shutters once more; barbers, musicians, waiters, and all the various people who found employment during the season had returned in a dudgeon to the metropolis.

The old gentleman continued his walk along the beautiful lakeside road, now strewn with fallen leaves, past villas whose shutters were bolted and barred. He went the same way every day. The bathing-huts were locked, the rowboats drawn up on the beach, the Navigation Company's large motor-boat traversed the sunny lake idly and alone. The natives sat about in indolence and bad temper. It was an insult to be given the promise of warm and peerless weather now when the summer was at an end. Who was there to make these beauties of nature pay? There were scarcely a hundred people in the whole place.

The little old gentleman strolled gently along with his air of importance, enjoying the pleasant warmth. The surface of the lake was barely broken with ripples of a tender hue. The wooded hills, the peaks behind, newly decked in

snow, were spotless in the calm sky. A gardener was tying
up plants with bast, a man in shirt-sleeves hammering up
a hut with large nails. They said good-day to the stranger.
To watch him go by was a welcome excuse for interrupting their mild activities. They grinned when he had
passed; his small size and self-importance and his frog's
mouth struck them as funny. They had found out already
all there was to know about him, and it was not much; you
couldn't with the best will in the world make a long story
of it. He was called Robert Wickersberg, took his meals
at the Hotel Mangart, and was staying at the Villa Kainzenhuber. There he had two rooms to himself, which he
had taken without even questioning the excessive price
Frau Kainzenhuber, the Privy Councillor's wife, asked for
them. If he had refused to pay it, the natives would have
abused him mercilessly; when he did, they laughed at him
for his innocence.

The old gentleman meanwhile arrived at the end of
the promenade, with his soft felt hat in his hand and the
wind playing about his white-thatched head, in which his
teeth, projecting at an angle, resembled roof tiles. Here
there was a small open space with seats and a bust of the
far-famed composer of songs, Matthias Laischacher, who

had been a native of the place. The old gentleman stopped in front of the bust and took a good look at it. The composer must have had a coarse, fleshy face with a plentiful moustache; and the bronze bust did not succeed in subduing the hopeless vulgarity of the man it represented. The composer had formed a quartet with three of his fellow-countrymen; he himself sang, and his quartet became famous; he had given recitals on both sides of the ocean, earning much money and many honours. The old gentleman regarded the bust earnestly without a smile while he pictured this man with his three colleagues, all in dress clothes, singing his tender melodies to a crowded concert hall. He pictured all this to himself still without a smile and without a smile read the bombastic inscription which paid honour in swelling words to the banal and sentimental music of a successful fellow-townsman.

A path branched off from the little open space around the bust, leading steeply up into the woods. It was lonely and uncared for. The old gentleman climbed up it. He had been longing for solitude and now he ardently embraced it. Yes, his name was Robert Wickersberg; but that, even though the inhabitants had never heard of it, was a far from obscure name. Robert Wickersberg passed as one of the few true poets of his country; with many, as the first among them. He lived austerely in the seclusion of a small town surrounded by a circle of devoted disciples. It was exacting to live year after year like that, expressing opinions each of which was authoritative; always being the first, always behaving accordingly, never shirking by word or gesture the onus of responsibility. Even though one had nothing but contempt for the opinion of the world, it seeped through; and even though newspapers were banished from the Presence, yet from the lips of disciples one heard what they contained. One lived in an ivory tower, but the world was still there below; it was in one's eye, and the sight of it fretted the soul. It was imperative to have a rest from it all, a respite from the domestic autocracy over one's following and from being constantly in the view, even though a distant view, of the world's judgment. So without warning, without a word to anyone of his destination, he came away to Vörtschau, suspecting that it was one of the few places in the whole country where his name was unknown.

Arriving at the eminence to which the path led, he sat down on the bench placed there to afford a view of the beautiful though not exhilarating prospect, and surveyed the mountains and the lake. It was the sixth day of his stay. He walked about among people who were slow, uncouth, avaricious, simple-minded—a great man whose eminence no one knew; he sat on benches here or there, lay under trees, swam, rowed. All in moderation, the same as at home. It was all just as he had expected, and yet not as he had expected. At home not a newspaper was allowed in his sight; here it was all he could do not to seize upon the local papers which lay about in the hotel. At home no stranger was permitted to cross his threshold, and his intimates counted their words lest they weary him. Here he talked every morning to his landlady, Frau Kainzenhuber, and at midday to the manager of the Hotel Mangart. Frau Kainzenhuber, since he was accustomed to drink tea, dwelt at length on the appetizing and beneficent qualities of Austrian coffee. The manager opened up on Austrian wine, of which the cheaper growths were particularly to be commended; and then on the bad season and all it meant, on the song composer Matthias Laischacher, of whom he possessed a score in the original manuscript. It was a tender melody, set to words which described the faithfulness till death of two lovers who set out at eve over the calm bosom of the lake. The manager had already thrice shown him this manuscript in its costly frame.

The poet Robert Wickersberg looked at his watch and walked back to the hotel for lunch. He was early, but in spite of this he found the sparse company already assembled. There was nothing to do here, particularly at this dead season, but wait from one meal to the next. Herr Wickersberg observed his fellow-guests. There were a few insignificant persons, petty officials and stenographers of the higher type; then there was a Jewish married couple from Vienna, a shrewd and effeminate-looking solicitor with an exuberant and vivacious wife; lastly, a family party who spoke Saxon, consisting of a well-dressed father, a haughty mother, and a young, loud, pretty daughter. It was clear that some of them had been asking each other about the man of the peculiar appearance. No doubt also they had discovered his name, but it was certain to mean nothing to them to know that it was Robert Wickersberg. He had persistently mocked at the opinion of the world; interviewers found him haughtily dumb, photographers invisible. And yet it rather dashed him that his name should mean nothing at all to these people.

After lunch he went to the bathing-establishment. It was utterly deserted. He got undressed. The skin of his well-cared-for body was still perfectly smooth. The bathing during the last few days had reddened it; tomorrow it would be tanned. Robert Wickersberg mounted to the gallery, anointed himself with oil, and lay down on the planks. He shut his eyes and, stretched out at full length, basked in the hot sun. The ripples plashed and from the distance he heard the hammering of the man who was nailing up the hut. An aeroplane came over at a great height; the sound of the engines was no more than a soft hum. It was the regular Vienna-Venice service. One might go to Venice again—but no, there would be people there who would recognize him. The flight here over the mountains from Vienna had been very beautiful. Really, being here was exactly what he wanted. The climate suited him; he had not felt so vigorous for years. He was sure his projects would thrive in the deliberately courted boredom of the place. His play *Asmodai,* of which two acts were completed, would come to something. He was not written out —not an old man by any means. Last century a man was done for at fifty or sixty. Today that was not the case. Human longevity—all the statistics proved it—was increasing. He had lived a healthy life—even though he might have drunk his share. But he had no thought of making his exit—far from it. They called the coloured and exquisite style of which he was master a thing of the past; but when a little more water had flowed under the bridge they would find that it alone had the stamp of immortality. Its adherents might not be many, but they would not diminish and they were the best. Even the reviewers knew that. The younger generation, the upstarts who made fun of him, had many illusions to live through yet. A few lean years—admitted; but now new life stirred in him. It would, after all, have been a bore if everything were already attained. It was just as well that something still remained to do. *Asmodai* would open their eyes—even Franz, the waiter's.

The face of the poet Wickersberg contracted at the thought of the waiter Franz. Franz was the thorn in his side. He was the headwaiter of the café which the poet had patronized for forty years and still, now that he was a celebrity, patronized every two months or so. Franz had been at the café for nearly the whole of the time and had much to thank the poet for—many clients, big tips, interviews in the papers. But Franz, and this was the worm

that ate into the poet's heart, had no belief in him. Franz
had heard the poet sharply criticized; there had been many
a fierce battle before Robert Wickersberg was enthroned
as the god of his circle; certain persons—some of whom
now belonged to the communion of believers while others
were banished for ever from it—had expressed their views
without picking their words. Franz had frequently gathered that Wickersberg's marmoreal verse was tripe. Had
Wickersberg been able to convince himself that these vulgar gibes were alone responsible for it, then Franz's unbe-
lief would have passed him by. But he knew well that
Franz had formed his own opinion, not at random, but
out of the matured judgment of a man with a wide knowledge of men. He had never expressed this opinion to the
poet's face. He was a well-trained waiter and knew his
place. But Wickersberg could read it in his eye and in the
manner with which Franz put his coffee down before him.
And though, as time went on, the sales of Wickersberg's
plays ran into thousands, though they were translated into
every language under the sun and even produced on the
stage in Japan, the waiter Franz was as polite, as atten-
tive, and as unconvinced as ever. Both knew it without a
word said. Only once, shortly after his fiftieth birthday,

when the homage of the whole world of letters still hung in a cloud of incense about the poet's knees, Wickersberg had asked: "Well, Franz, still nothing to say?" But the waiter merely looked back at him in distress and regretfully raised his shoulders.

This, then, was what passed through the poet's mind in the deserted bathing-establishment of Vörtschau; and the poet's mind was vexed. But the sun melted his annoyance. He thought of the verses about the desert in his play of Solomon and Asmodai, the verses in which the yellow expanses of the desert were caught for all time. He lay on the warm planks of the gallery; his well-preserved, though no longer youthful body gleamed with oil and a light perspiration, and he was filled with an exquisitely pleasant indolence.

Someone else arrived. Robert Wickersberg raised himself on one elbow and peeped through the balustrade. It was the little Saxon girl he had seen in the restaurant. She had come in bathing-dress and cloak. She looked up and smiled, expecting him to say something. But he said nothing, so she stayed below and lay down in the sun.

The little Saxon girl was pretty, charming, and slender. Her eyes were long and narrow and of a deep, rather stupid blue, and she had a nice laugh. But what did she matter? He was possessed now by his pleasant indolence, and, besides, there were his plans to ponder. He was in good form; he was going to give his detractors something to think of. They were good plans.

They were wretched plans. *Asmodai* might possibly have come to something. His vision at the time had been clear, the colours strong and rich. Without affectation, he had found his feet when the king put the demon on the throne in his own place and himself descended among the last of men on the edge of the desert in order to experience human life to the bottom. He had written the first act right off at one go. It was good stuff and came unforced out of the fullness of his inspiration. So far, his vision had flowed and flowered. But he got no further. The sail had flapped against the mast and there it still flapped. Three times, four times, he had set to work. Once a breeze sprang up and that yellow song of the desert came into his mind. But for the rest, no melody had come; it was laboured, dry, without impetus. No one but himself would know it. He had the hand of a master; even dull and soulless clay shaped by his hand took on the sheen of marble. But it was clay all the same and he knew it.

Be that as it might—the desert verses were good, verses of his own brand, the brand of his best years. Let the upstarts of today try and do the like. He stretched himself in the sun, dried the pleasant light perspiration, anointed himself afresh, turned on the other side, laid his head on his bent arm. The days here had done him good. It was here the verses of the desert had come to him. He had chosen well: Vörtschau at this season was the very place for him. Its inhabitants were a smug and money-grubbing lot, hard and dull; all the same it was a good place, and one day they would say: "Here Robert Wickersberg wrote his play *Solomon and Asmodai.*"

He might really venture to give himself rope. He might venture to glance at a newspaper now and then, perhaps even have a word with the Saxon girl. He was so little tempted by life in its lower manifestations that a sniff or two at it merely emphasized the salubrious abstinence of his days in his native land. He got up and went to the balustrade. Yes, there she was, still lying in the sun, slender and pretty in her bathing-suit. He descended the steps. She turned her head and eyed him through the slits of her eyes. He walked past her and her gaze very lazily followed him. He sprinkled himself in order to accustom himself to the coolness and then cautiously stepped down into the water and swam about for a few minutes. Then he got out of the water again and gave himself a good shake. Then he went up the steps to the gallery, wrapped himself in his bathing-cloak, and leaning over the rail, looked down upon the Saxon girl who still lay in the same spot in the sun.

Suddenly she said, blinking indolently: "Why on earth didn't you dive in?"

He, feeling foolish and not knowing quite what to reply, finally hedged: "I think my way is more sensible."

"I should find it a bore—creeping in an inch at a time," she observed.

After this they exchanged a few more aimless remarks. She spoke a very strong Saxon and what she said was inane. But the poet somehow found her more intelligent, and the way she luxuriated in the sun was a charming sight. Without warning she took the offensive.

"What on earth do you find to do at Vörtschau?" she asked. "I should think a grown man would perish of boredom here."

"Perhaps," he said, "I wish to be bored."

"Oh—by talking to me? You're very polite," she remarked tartly.

Wickersberg took no offence at her Saxon ways.

"Why are you here yourself if you find it a bore?" he asked.

She told him without hesitation that she had been unable to induce her parents to choose a livelier place. Her father, a Dresden manufacturer, had to have peace and nature for his holidays. The best she had been able to do was to get him to promise to take her to Venice in a fortnight's time. Suddenly she sprang nimbly to her feet and, saying she was too hot, took a header into the lake.

She was out again in a moment and joined him, squealing and splashing.

Robert Wickersberg knew that the smiles women gave him were generally because of his achievements, his name and success, perhaps his influence. It gladdened him that he now found favour with the girl merely as Herr Wickersberg, that she was attracted to him even when he did not stand on the pedestal of his fame.

She sat confidingly beside him, looking very pretty in her wet bathing-dress, and told him all about herself. Her parents were prosperous, but it was just too boring to live as the model daughter of the house with no prospect other than a conventional marriage. She took lessons in singing and aspired to get to Berlin. There, with her looks, she would certainly land on her feet. Probably her parents would capitulate when they saw she really meant it. She told him all this in a single outburst, in her funny Saxon. Wickersberg listened. She spoke sensibly: she didn't believe she had great talent, but she could surely hold her own with the ordinary musical comedy girl. "Or do you think I'm not pretty enough for a Berlin revue?" She really was very pretty. Her name was Ilse.

They agreed to take a stroll together after dinner. Her parents would probably be tired; if not, they must, whatever happened, be left to trot on behind. So now they had a little plot between them.

Wickersberg had gone to Vörtschau in a listless mood. His successes had ceased to cheer him and he found no pleasure even in the lack of success of younger men. He took no joy in writing and none in reading. The placid lake was no pleasure to him, nor the clean line of the mountains, nor the sense of his own well-preserved vigour. But now he went back through the town with a quicker step. He embarked on a conversation with the woman who sold fruit at the corner. He bought Vienna papers at the little general store. He read the gossip with interest, cheered by a malicious anecdote about a fellow-writer and a reverent mention of his own name. He took a seat on the promenade, beating time with his soft and shapely hand, to a melody which had come into his mind. Natives who passed by shook their heads and wrote him off as balmy.

He returned to his rooms and shaved himself for the second time, changed his coat and collar, and spoke a few words to old Frau Kainzenhuber with such an engaging air that she found him for once quite the gentleman and really affable. During dinner he entered into intimate conversation with the manager and flattered him still further by a request to be shown once again the manuscript of the composer Matthias Laischacher. He drank the palatable Austrian wine, and made an antiquated observation to the strapping, vivacious waitress which had a faint echo of gallantry about it. She took it up with a tactful laugh.

At last came the assignation for the after-dinner stroll. The parents, after a slight recalcitrance, trotted on ahead somewhere, and he found himself left in the darkness with the Saxon girl. But she had altered since the afternoon; she was wayward and antagonistic. He realized with bitterness that he was a white-haired owl. She asked him what he did when he was at home. He wrote, he replied without committing himself further.

"If you write for the newspapers," she said, "you might be some use to me."

When he did not take this hint, she decided he was bragging and became extremely sharp.

He saw that he would not make a good impression unless he appealed to his books, but shame deterred him when he was on the point of trying to enlighten her. Had he come to this little retreat to start a foolish flirtation with a girl who was no different from a thousand others of her kind? Her Saxon father was fully justified if he laughed at him for a white-haired old fool. The poet sank into silence.

"You're tired and boring," the Saxon girl informed him with a sniff.

Next day he was again the petulant, lonely old gentleman. He went for a walk, gazed for a long while and with disgust at the bust of Laischacher, the composer of songs, rowed on the lake. Later he came upon the Saxon girl at the bathing-station. But she was not alone. Beside her in a bathing-gown lay a young man who, in Herr Wickersberg's opinion, appeared arrogant and loud. The girl was laughing excitedly and there was no doubt at all that they were getting on very well indeed. The poet lay down above, as on the day before. Probably she was making fun of him for the benefit of that rather vulgar youth. She was perfectly at liberty to do so. In any case it was a matter of utter indifference to him. He shut his eyes. Delightful to lie in the sun—it would be even more delightful if one had the sun entirely to oneself. The noisy chatter of those young people disturbed him.

After awhile he went down to have a swim. The Saxon girl called out to him. This led to a little talk in which the young man joined with the amiable politeness of an Austrian. They spoke of bathing and of the charm of the little island which lay opposite. During the season a café was open there, and people rowed out to it, swimming a good part of the way. They discussed whether it would be too much to swim the whole distance. The young man said that for him it would be nothing at all. Herr Wickersberg said that he was a fairly strong swimmer himself, though out of training at the moment. The Saxon girl looked at him with her narrow, dark-blue eyes and then looked at the youth. "It's easy to talk," she said.

"Do you think," asked Wickersberg, "that I couldn't swim it?"

Again she looked from him to the youth and shrugged her shoulders. She looked charmingly slender and youthful in her bathing-suit.

Robert Wickersberg descended the wooden steps into the lake. One of the steps was shaky and he was precipitated rather ludicrously into the water. The girl laughed. The poet swam a few trial strokes and turned over on his back. The afternoon was getting on. The water was not exactly warm. It was easy to tell that autumn had come. The Saxon girl and the youth leant on the rail and shouted some remark after him. He headed for the island.

He swam with an easy, regular stroke and then lay on his back and rested. He was really a practised swimmer and had covered long distances in southern seas. The water of this Alpine lake had certainly less buoyancy and it was also devilish cold. He swam more quickly to keep himself warm. He enjoyed the physical sensation of the water and the movement, and had long since forgotten the Saxon girl. He was now quite close to the island. He turned over again and lay with his eyes shut, gently rocking on the surface with a solemn, childish expression on his face; above were the sparse white clouds of an evening sky. Then he swam the last stretch and proudly strode ashore with as much pride as if he had pulled off the final act of *Asmodai*. Very soon he felt strangely cold and began to shiver. It was disgusting to have that stupid café closed just then. He ran to and fro and made violent movements of the arms. The stones and pebbles hurt his naked feet. But he could not get warm.

He went back into the lake with repugnance. It was dusk and really cold. He swam quickly and strongly with his chin sunk in the water. Then he told himself he would have to husband his strength. Out and forward— steady. He decided to count three hundred strokes and then return to the crawl for a bit. But in spite of the cold he had to rest. Otherwise he would never do it. The wind in his face was detestable; no peace from those beastly ripples breaking against his ears and mouth. It was costing him a good quarter of an hour having the wind against him. The shore seemed to retreat farther and farther instead of drawing any nearer. There was surely a current taking him out of his course. It was quite dark by this time. The devil only knew how long he had been swimming. Disgusting. But he must not hurry. He must control himself. No squandering of strength and time. That light there must never leave his eye. Not an inch must he deviate from his course, not a single unnecessary movement must he make. Thus he laboured on in the cold and darkness, regularly, quietly, breathing hard, with beating heart and neck extended.

He was blue with cold when he gripped the steps that led up to the bathing-station; he was shivering violently and it was all he could do to pull himself up to the level of the railings. He stood with panting sides. His face was glazed and stiff as he tried to chafe his arms and legs. It was night; there was not a soul about; the Saxon girl and the youth had long since gone. The lake was black and sinister. A wind and no moon.

Robert Wickersberg pulled on his clothes as fast as he could and went home. He asked Frau Kainzenhuber, who mildly upbraided him, for some hot wine and went to bed. He slept badly; he felt feverish and limp. He decided not to get up next day. By midday his temperature was so high that Frau Kainzenhuber became anxious and called in a neighbour. It was decided to have the old gentleman taken to the hospital at Kaltenfurth, a small town near by.

One of the younger house surgeons had a taste for reading. The name Wickersberg was familiar to him. He observed the remarkable, frog-mouthed head of the sick man and was convinced that the patient and the poet were one and the same.

Next day the local paper announced that the well-known poet and writer, Robert Wickersberg, who had been taking a rest cure at Vörtschau, lay seriously ill with inflammation of the lungs in Kaltenfurth hospital; there was, however, every hope that the proven skill of the Kaltenfurth doctors would save the life of their distinguished visitor. The news appeared that evening in the Vienna press; the morning after it was known to the world.

The good people of Vörtschau instantly forgot that they had ever laughed at the peculiar old gentleman with his frog's mouth and teeth like roof-tiles. Every hotel and inn in Kaltenfurth and the parish of Vörtschau had its complement of busy journalists from Vienna, who rooted round in every corner to find out how the sick man had spent his days, whom he had talked to, and what had brought him to Vörtschau, of all places. They took up their posts in and around the little hospital, gaping for news, like the fishes at the lake's edge when visitors threw them crumbs, each one eager to be the first to give the distressing news to his paper. The doctors who were in charge of the rapidly failing man had to issue a bulletin every half-hour; the little post office requested reinforcements from Vienna. Some of the journalists were the common run of sceptical and cynical human being. Some were not unmoved when they telegraphed the news that there was now little or no prospect of the patient's recovery, and there were others who thought it quite time the old fellow made his bow.

It was a perfect early autumn. Vörtschau, which was now mentioned more frequently in the papers than other resorts, began to attract visitors. The café once again set out its tables right down to the edge of the lake; the Navigation Company brought out its second large motor-boat; and the lake was dotted with skiffs. Who would ever have thought that the pavilion La Gloriette would have been so well patronized again that year? The man in shirt-sleeves pulled out the nails with which he had boarded up his hut; the instructor appeared once more at the bathing-station. The affiliated musical societies of Kaltenfurth and Vörtschau joined forces in rehearsing

some of the more solemn melodies of the composer Laischacher. The manager of the Hotel Mangart was particularly in evidence. He had his second pair of striped
trousers pressed with all speed, and was never tired of telling, with all the flourishes of Austrian politeness, how en-
grossed and how interested the Master had been by the
conversations they had had, how charmed he had been by
the lake, the mountains, the exhilarating air, and the hotel's
excellent Austrian cuisine. He lamented and deplored in
his guttural Carinthian speech the malignance of Fortune
in cutting the Master off in the midst of a rest cure which
could nowhere be bettered. He also expatiated with feeling
on the reverent eagerness with which the Master had again
and again asked to be shown the manuscript of the composer Laischacher. Often, with an earnest expression on his
face, sunk in meditation, he had stood for minutes together
before the bronze bust of the great musician. The gardener,
too, was always ready to tell, every day with fresh details,
what an interest the old gentleman had taken in his
flowers; it had been easy to see that this was no common
visitor, that there was something special about him. In
fact, recollecting the words of one of Laischacher's songs,
the gardener insisted on sending the sick man a bunch of

Michaelmas daisies and his last roses. But Frau Kainzenhuber had more to say than all the rest. She offered the
reporters a cup of her excellent Austrian coffee and told
them she had divined from the first moment that a great
man had come to her modest but admirably kept and
superior house. She had, however, been as reasonable as
possible and in spite of her conviction that coffee was more
wholesome had with particular care and with her own
hands made him the tea he was so obstinately set on. All
these details were dished up again and again for the newspapers. They had to be carefully husbanded, for the patient
was intolerably slow in dying; it was positively a disgrace
the way he kept a man hanging about.

Meanwhile, Robert Wickersberg lay in the best room
of the Kaltenfurth hospital. It was clear to him most of
the time that his end had come. But he did not hurry; he
was not going to be hustled. He was often delirious and
saw visions of one kind or other. Once he saw the missing
end of his *Asmodai* as he had seen it when the work first
leapt freshly into his mind. It did not vex him that in spite
of this clear vision the play would probably never be completed. On the contrary, he smiled slyly when he considered that now no producer and no company and no

profiteers would scramble for it, that rather, unknown to anyone, it would slip with him from the world. His only regret was that neither would the waiter Franz know anything about it and would so keep to his mistaken opinion of Wickersberg's merit.

Wickersberg's divorced wife came. She had great expectations of this death-bed scene, but she was deceived. The poet received her with coolness and she was not received a second time. Even the reporters made little of her. Frau Wickersberg had already made a chatty and rather too out-spoken book of the grievance she nursed in her heart against the poet. It was an old story; it had no news value. The newspapers were more concerned to have the observation of Frau Kainzenhuber and the manager of the hotel.

Wickersberg lay in bed feeling limp, disheartened— sometimes, too, a little cheated by God and the world. Often as the opportunities had presented themselves, he had not valued enough the charm of flirting with a woman, of showing himself with pride and scorn to an audience he had overwhelmed, of drinking good wine by the edge of a beautiful lake. Now he would not be sorry to crowd many days with such pleasures, however besotted they might be. Quite apart from *Asmodai*. How good it would be to write it to the end! But sixty comes, and if you get so far, eighty, and even so, what is it but toil and trouble?

Then it occurred to him how it was that he had so nearly succeeded in finishing *Asmodai*. He knew of a sudden who the girl of the desert was from whom the play had caught its subdued glow. It was decades since he had seen her; perhaps she was dead long ago, but he knew exactly the turn of her head—lean and slender and a little sharp. He saw her in the long, old-fashioned blue dress she wore when he first met her at the suburban dance long ago. For he was young in those days; and although it was only in a derisive and ironical mood that he had accompanied a friend of his to that provincial entertainment, he was still a long way from the severity which cramped his later years; and he had looked at this girl in blue very much more attentively than he had at the Saxon girl Ilse. He had not been in her company very often and yet now in the hospital at Kaltenfurth he had a vivid memory of the large pores in her hand, of her worn brown shoes, of her rather too high-pitched voice and of her whole slight figure, which in those days seemed to him so radiant and alert. Probably she might have been all that; but she had missed her decade, she had come too soon.

A decade later she would have been sent to college or given a career of some kind. As it was she had some office job and no doubt had soured there. When he took his walk with the Saxon girl Ilse the other day, it was only because something about the carriage of her head reminded him of that thin, sharp girl. Really it was a pity he had never bothered over the girl in blue. No, it was not a pity. It would certainly have ended in a disillusionment. As it was there was that subdued glow in the desert girl of his play *Asmodai*.

It would be disgusting if strange eyes read their own vulgarity into this girl of the desert. He realized without anger how little, for example, that utterly unimaginative Ilse would make of her. He had his papers brought him. He made the nurse pick out in his presence all that belonged to *Asmodai*. Then she had to write a letter for him to the waiter Franz Klüsgens, in the little Rhineland town, asking him on receipt of the letter to telegraph his promise that he would never say a word to anybody about the packet which Robert Wickersberg proposed to send him. Then he told her to destroy this letter and simply tie up the sheets of *Asmodai* she had picked out, seal the packet, and then write on a label: "To be delivered after my death to Herr Franz Klüsgens, waiter at B. on the Rhine." Robert Wickersberg signed the label and made her promise secrecy. He **no** longer needed Franz's promise. He saw the broad, reliable, peasant face of the nurse, and the thought that his last success would come into the hands of Franz, the waiter, instead of into those of a rag-dealer filled him with a crafty joy. It was a time of happiness, the best time of his life, perhaps, apart from the time he had spent with the girl in the blue dress, and it was a long time, almost a quarter of an hour long. Then at last the stern and hopeless struggle for life set in.

Ilse, the Saxon girl, was put out when she learnt who it was that had swum across to the island in her honour. So the old gentleman was a great man—Robert Wickersberg, the poet; not so celebrated as a boxer or a tennis champion, but well known all the same. Actually it was for her he had died. For a whole afternoon she gave herself up to the confusion of her feelings, eating nothing, drinking nothing, seeing nothing of the young man. It saddened even more than disgusted her not to have known who Robert Wickersberg was. Probably, if she had only set her mind on it, he would have made her his wife, or at least his mistress.

The next day she came to the conclusion that to have had him die for her was really even more *chic*. She explained this to the reporters. Very soon she was Robert Wickersberg's last love. The poet's divorced wife paled before her and a literary magazine compared the Saxon Ilse with Ulrike von Levetzow, the last love of the poet J. W. von Goethe. Her Dresden parents concluded that no resistance could now be offered to the artistic destiny of their daughter, and Saxon Ilse, as Robert Wickersberg's last mistress, had a magnificent spring-board for her career.

The interment of the poet Wickersberg was an event whose importance recalled the interment of the composer Laischacher. Representatives of the Government, of important public bodies and the theatrical world, were there. The affiliated musical societies of Kaltenfurth and Vörtschau honoured the great man's memory by a recital of certain tender and moving songs. All the newspapers gave lengthy reports, also numerous pictures.

All this drew public attention to Vörtschau and its lake. The autumn season made an astonishing spurt. The parish council decided to put up a bust of the poet Wickersberg on the little open space at the end of the promenade, opposite the bust of their own celebrity, Laischacher.

HERR HANNSICKE'S SECOND BIRTH

HERR HANNSICKE'S
SECOND BIRTH

Franz G. Hannsicke, a rather bleak young man with a long, pimply face and inflamed, spectacled eyes, was standing in his room in Borsigstrasse one December evening. The room was painted green and contained a bed, a table, and two chairs—representing the cheapest lines of Davidsohn & Sons, the furniture makers. Besides these there was a small and flimsy bookshelf, a wireless set, and a birdcage—whose inmate, however, was by this time dead. Franz G. Hannsicke was fed up and tired. He was in favour of a diet rich in vitamins, a believer in the doctrine of the survival of the fittest and in supermen, a member of a political party which engaged in propaganda work for a dictatorship and also of a rational footwear society. By profession he was a bookseller's assistant. He took little pleasure in his profession, for people would not buy the authors he favoured, and when he pressed upon them the war memoirs of a hero or Nietzsche's *Zarathustra,* the customer replied that he wanted the book where the scene was laid in East Prussia in a green binding but it must not cost more than 3.50 marks. And so, disillusioned by his occupation, embittered by the refusal of an advance in salary which would have enabled him to buy a new suit and in consequence to be elected to the committee of his society; galled, further, by his girl's jilting him because for lack of money he had had to invite her three times in succession to go for a walk instead of to a place of entertainment; exasperated, finally, by the inadequate heating of his room, Franz G. Hannsicke decided—when, to top it all, the match with which he was about to light the gas wouldn't strike—to make no further attempt but simply to turn the gas on and his life off without more ado.

The gas escaped with a gentle singing hiss as soon as Franz G. Hannsicke had turned on the tap, which he was able to see quite clearly in the broad shaft of light cutting the room in an unpleasant slant from the street lamp outside. Next Franz G. Hannsicke had a feeling of defiance and triumphant exhilaration. Without hesitation he had taken the first important step in his life and he was in no mood to listen any longer to nonsense about fate. He wondered what the landlady, with whom he had daily trouble over the scrape of butter on his bread, would say; what the bookseller who had turned down his request for a rise would think. He inhaled the sickly smell as it grew stronger and stronger and tried to calculate how long it would take, looked at his watch, stepping for this purpose into the track of light. Then he considered what a pity it was—a young fellow like himself, intellectual, gifted, and full of the best intentions. The whole fault lay with the bad organization of society and what was wanted was a dictator. What would his funeral be like? He imagined the paragraph in the newspapers; the *Anzeiger,* of course, would barely give him a line, probably without even the mention of his name. He thought he felt a slight dizziness, though perhaps it was only imagination. A vision of men with gas-masks on rose before his eyes. He took off his spectacles; it seemed more dignified to die without his spectacles. He repeated to himself: "The undiscover'd country, from whose bourne no traveller returns," and wondered whether he should lie down on his bed or whether it would be more suitable to arrive in that country seated on a chair. He thought: "Death and the Fool"—this was the title of a book of which he had sold several copies. There had been a violent scene between him and his employer because of one copy which a customer was determined to return and he was determined not to take back. Then it occurred to him that this month's gas bill would be pretty high and that the landlady would certainly indemnify herself out of his belongings. It was very sad, he felt, to be dying alone like this; he longed for the sight of a human face and went to the window with a step that was already uncertain—he felt sure—but the people in the street below went silently through the snow like ghosts, as though he were already seeing them in the other world. He heard an indistinct noise from the wireless set and went across to it, positively dragging himself along—it seemed to him—and put the earphones over his projecting ears.

He heard a broad, good-natured provincial voice, discoursing about tortoises. It was odd to think that the last one was to hear of this world was details of the life of tortoises—all the same it was better to pass out to the accompaniment of the human voice than with empty ears. The very small skull, the voice said, was occupied by a brain whose size held no proportion at all to the size of the body. Tortoises weighing ninety pounds had a brain that did not weigh one-seventh of an ounce. Tortoises were among the oldest inhabitants of this planet. They could stand extreme

heat and drought, but not great cold. Their muscular
strength was amazing. A medium-sized land tortoise could
carry a boy seated astride on its back. A really large one
could carry several men at once for long distances without
trouble. They could survive for incredibly long periods without eating, and indeed without breathing. Even after the
most frightful mutilation they continued to function for
months exactly as though they were uninjured. Their vital-
ity was so tremendous that in the Botanical Gardens of
Paris a mud turtle lived for six years without nourishment.

The book salesman Franz G. Hannsicke, with the earphones still over his projecting ears, dragging the instrument after him, and breathing hard through his nose, this
time really tottered to the window, threw it open, drew a
deep breath, walked back, and turned off the gas-cock.
He felt a slight nausea but also a sense of overwhelming
exaltation and ravenous hunger. There was still a faint
sweetish smell in the room and there still came a voice from
the wireless set. He pulled on his thin shabby overcoat. Now
for a glass of beer or perhaps even wine and then to a dance-
hall to look for another girl. As he left the flat his landlady
came in. "Did you know," he shouted cheerily at her, "that
a tortoise could carry several men on its back?" The woman

thought he was being personal and made an abusive rejoinder.

Meanwhile, the broad, good-natured slightly provincial voice concluded its discourse on tortoises. Tortoises, it said, were greatly sinned against; for people wrongly took their powers of endurance to be a sign of unwavering health. But the tortoise was highly sensitive to influences it scarcely seemed to feel. Only it suffered very slowly. And from this it was falsely assumed that it could endure anything.

THE
ARMOURED CRUISER
''ORLOV''

THE ARMOURED CRUISER "ORLOV"

While at this early hour all the other cinemas in Berlin were either shut or very meagrely patronized, the approach to this one was blocked by cars and policemen and loafers. The film—*The Armoured Cruiser "Orlov"*—had been shown thirty-six times already, four times a day; thirty-six thousand Berliners had seen it. Yet people were as excited as though they were the first to be shown something for which the world was waiting.

Klenk, the cabinet minister, who towered head and shoulders above everyone sitting near him, had no intention of being infected by the agitation around him. He had read that it was a film without construction, without love interest, without plot, in which story was replaced by propaganda. He had to see the thing since he was in Berlin. But he was not going to let these Jews take him in with their cleverly exploited sensations.

First, a few bars of strident and chaotic music, *fortissimo*.

Then, secret documents from the files of the Admiralty, from which it appeared that on a certain date the crew of the cruiser *Orlov* had mutinied off Odessa on account of insufficient rations. All right—they mutinied. As a boy he had read such tales with avidity. Very interesting in the later years of adolescence. Klenk grinned.

The men's sleeping-quarters. Hammocks crowded one beside another. An officer nosing about among the restlessly sleeping sailors. All quite cleverly done. You could almost smell the bad air. Then that heavy stupefying music.

Now—the morning. Sailors collecting round a hanging piece of meat. They look at it distastefully. More and more come up. It needs only a sniff to tell them that it does not smell good. A close-up of the bit of meat: it is seething with maggots. It seems the crew has often enough had meat of that sort. They curse—very naturally. The ship's doctor is brought in. He puts his pince-nez on his nose with a fussy air and does his duty by examining the meat and finding nothing wrong with it. The meat is cooked. The crew refuses to touch the stuff. More cursing. A few trivial incidents follow, baldly presented without much snap. You have the stinking meat, the sailors, the officers. Not particularly capable officers, it appears, nor on the other hand particularly bad ones. Just the common run. We have much the same in Bavaria, Klenk thought to himself. Odd, though, that he was stirred by those very ordinary fellows and very ordinary occurrences.

The bad feeling on the ship increases, you hardly know how or why. But you realize, and everyone of the audience realizes, that there is trouble brewing. The officers on the screen are not taking it seriously enough. They ought to do something about it, in fact, put a stop to it. Are they blind? But we saw the same thing coming in the last year of the war and did nothing till it was too late. True, we didn't have this pounding music. It's appalling, this music, but you can't escape it. Of course a film like this ought to be stopped. It's nothing but deliberate propaganda, scandalous. A bit of maggoty meat is no reason for throwing all discipline to the winds. We had much worse than that to swallow in the war, my friends. All the same, Klenk is not altogether on the officers' side. He is for the sailors.

The thudding, menacing music goes on and on. The ferment increases. The captain has the crew lined up on deck and asks if any man has any complaint to make of the rations. After a pause one or two step forward. Instantly, before you realize it, the malcontents, the ringleaders, the best men of the crew, are separated from their fellows. There is a wide and ominous space set between them and the rest. Those officers are smart fellows after all. In the twinkling of an eye they have the instigators of the mutiny in their power. The main body of the crew stands in a frightened huddle. The small group of leaders is roped off, penned in a corner, and in a moment a bit of sailcloth is thrown over them. You can see it billowing with their absurd helpless movements. Rifle barrels are levelled at it. A cry escapes from the throat of one of the crew and immediately after comes the command: "Fire!" But no one fires. The rifles are silent.

Frenzy—on the screen and in front of it. Why have they waited so long? Now we have it, now they're up in arms, now it's begun. The people in front of the screen are jubilant and cheer the men on the screen. Their clapping accompanies the hideous, exultant, thudding, horrible music as they see the officers madly hunted down, hauled out of their silly hiding-places, and hurled overboard into the joyfully leaping waves—one after the other, the fussy doctor among them, pince-nez and all.

Klenk sat motionless. His breathing had stopped. His great bulk was as still as a mouse. He had no thought of intervening. There it was, as sure as he breathed; it was the sober fact in the real world, and it was folly to deny it. You had to look on, you had to hear the music; there was no stopping it now.

The flag is hauled down, another run up to the masthead —a red flag—amid shouts of uproarious enthusiasm. Sailors take the place of the officers; and the ship performs none the worse. It makes for Odessa harbour flying the red flag.

At first the town is of two minds about the red flag; then it greets it with a cheer. Everyone breathes more quickly; everyone is jubilant; a great oppression is lifted. They board the ship with its red flag, at first singly, then in crowds; the whole town goes on a pilgrimage to the body of the one sailor who has been shot and whose body has been brought ashore; boats swarm round the ship and its red flag; people take the sailors supplies of food from their own not very plentiful stock.

Klenk began to feel uneasy. Were those others going to take this sitting down? Weren't they going to do something? He was not on their side; he was too quick-blooded to be unmoved by the impetuous surge of these events. It was simply that the realism of it, so perfect up to now, was suffering from this oversight. He was vexed that it should not be kept up.

But look—it is going to be kept up. There they are, the others. They have not been asleep and now they have come.

A flight of steps of enormous width which seems to have no end, and up it in a continuous procession the populace thronging to show the mutineers its sympathy—but not for long, for now those others, too, are on the steps. Down they come in open order—Cossacks with rifles, slowly and threateningly and irresistibly, barring the whole extent of the steps. The people waver and then quicken their pace; they break and take flight. Some, though, notice nothing and understand nothing; they hesitate in amazement. Meanwhile the soldiers' huge boots slowly descend, a step at a time, and smoke can be seen leaving the muzzles of their rifles. There is no more running on the steps—it's a wild stampede as long as legs and lungs hold out. But some just roll down; it is no longer force of will or legs or lungs that move them, but the force of gravity. They are dead. The boots of the Cossacks tramp on and on, and more and more of the people collapse and roll to the bottom. A woman who was pushing a perambulator is pushing it no longer. What's happened to her you do not know. But the peram-

bulator goes on alone, down landing after landing, until at
last at the tenth it comes to a stop. And after it, very large
and very slow, come the boots of the Cossacks.

They have not been asleep out at sea either. Large and
powerful ships have come on the scene, and the *Orlov* is
surrounded. The *Orlov* clears for action. The great barrels of its guns, shining like glass, are directed upwards and
downwards, gaping like dragons' throats. The needles of
the range-finders are in frantic activity. The great iron
creatures of destruction, powerful, perfect in every detail,
advance in a half-moon. The *Orlov* steams towards them.
She is faced by vessels of her own class, six, eight, ten of
them. There is no hope of breaking through and her guns
carry no farther than theirs. Victory is out of the question.
She can only perish after exacting the price of her destruction. On the screen and in front of it there is a wild, a heavy
suspense as the great ships close in round the *Orlov*.

The condemned ship begins to signal. Small bright-
coloured flags fluttering up and down to give the signal:
"Brothers, don't fire!" She steams slowly towards her pur-
suers signalling: "Don't fire!" The suspense becomes intolerable; you can hear everyone breathing round you.
"Don't fire!" is the hope, the prayer, the desire, into which

all the eight hundred people in this Berlin cinema put all the strength of their hearts.

Klenk could scarcely be called a tenderhearted, peace-loving man. He would have laughed outright if anyone had thought him that. He was a brutal, aggressive fellow who had no use for sentiment. Yet what passed through his mind as the mutinous ship moved on towards those loaded guns? He, too, with all the fierce strength of his heart, prayed: "Don't fire!"

When the *Orlov* was allowed to pass through the encircling ships, when unharmed she reached a neutral port, the oppression was lifted and every heart rejoiced.

Klenk, the cabinet minister, found himself in a confused state of mind he had never before experienced as he flung his heavy cloak round his shoulders, jammed his felt hat down on his great head, and issued from the cavernous gloom of the cinema into the open daylight of the street. What was it all about? Did it mean that he himself would not have opened fire on the mutineers? How could a man like himself have uttered that prayer—"Don't fire"? Well, there it was. Such films could be stopped, but it would not alter the fact that such things could happen and there was no sense in blinking it.

"ORLOV"

He saw his face in a shop window and caught a look of helplessness on it he had never seen before—like that of an animal in a trap. What was it all about? His face was not itself. He laughed self-consciously and then, after hailing a taxi, he knocked out his pipe, filled and lit it. By that time his face was set again in its old lines of fiercely complacent self-esteem.

HISTORY
OF THE
BRAIN SPECIALIST
DR. BL.

HISTORY OF THE
BRAIN SPECIALIST DR. BL.

The brain specialist Dr. Bl. was highly respected by his colleagues. His great reputation was due above all to the exactness of his researches, to the incorruptibility with which he traced important and desired conclusions back to the remotest sources of possible error. Anyone else with his gifts would have made a career for himself. He continued to occupy his chair at a small university. The fault lay with his caustic temperament. Perhaps it was his odd appearance that made him so cantankerous; for he carried a gigantic bearded head on a diminutive trunk. His manner towards his colleagues was marked by indifference, sometimes by positive dislike. Except to talk shop he scarcely ever opened his mouth, and if he did he was uncompromising in his opinions, terse and to the point in his comments on the world about him. Moreover, when well past his youth, he married a woman of an inferior station in life; she was a waitress in the restaurant where he used to snatch his hurried meals. He made no concealment of the fact that he felt happier in his wife's society than in that of his estimable colleagues.

Thus his fiftieth birthday came and went without causing any remark, and it seemed that he would descend, after closing his days without distinction, to an undistinguished grave. But suddenly the rumour spread that Professor Bl. had made a discovery which might be expected to give a new turn to life throughout the entire world. It was not easy to ascertain how the rumour arose. Presumably Dr. Bl. had spoken to a younger scientist of the instrument upon which he was working; no more than a hint probably. But a hint from him, as even his enemies allowed, was likely to have more foundation than the arrogant assertions of other men in scientific reports or other such publications. Professor Bl. had, if rumour was to be trusted, constructed an apparatus by means of which it was possible to take observations of the cerebral activity of living persons with such accuracy as to give an estimate of a person's intelligence. The instrument came to be called the intelligence-photometer.

The medical journals discussed Dr. Bl.'s invention, and soon the daily papers took it up. Many prominent men of the political, economic, and scientific worlds read about the intelligence-photometer with distinct uneasiness. Literary, artistic, and musical personages, on the other hand, were undismayed; for it was the fashion of the day to ask nothing more of them than a mysterious, nebulous something which was called creativeness but was not susceptible of further definition and had certainly nothing to do with intelligence. Professor Bl. maintained an obstinate silence.

Perhaps it was precisely this silence of his that made people talk more and more and with ever-increasing excitement about the intelligence-photometer—until at last it even came to the ears of the Dictator of the country.

He summoned the physiologist to his presence. Dr. Bl. regarded the Dictator as a species of gifted, undeveloped boy, whose gifts had certainly suffered from the exercise of power; for Dr. Bl. shared the opinion of the German philosopher that power makes people stupid. Small, informal, and bearded, he confronted the man whose brazen, domineering mask was adopted by his country as the symbol of greatness.

The Dictator was accustomed in his dealings with people to put on a stiff and heroic air. But he saw at once that it would not impress this testy dwarf, and as he had the sense of style, he adopted a matter-of-fact, everyday manner. This did not quite come off, but the little man noted the attempt with grim satisfaction.

"They tell me," said the Dictator, coming to the point at once, "that by means of your instrument you can measure a person's intelligence by a numerical scale and fix its limits." He sat massively behind his enormous desk, but his voice came lightly from his well-formed lips. "Can you do that?" he asked casually.

Professor Bl. answered: "Yes, I can," just as casually.

Naturally the Dictator was at first sceptical. The long expert opinion which lay before him was cautiously phrased, neither credulous nor incredulous. Perhaps it was the professor's casual, precise tone that swept away the Dictator's disbelief.

"That is a possibility," he said civilly, "which might have great importance for the welfare of the state and the nation."

Professor Bl. was silent, clearly because the remark was too obvious a one to merit a reply. The Dictator did not find conversation with this sea-urchin very easy. The simplest way was to be direct with him.

"And so," he went on dryly, "if I send certain men to

you, you can furnish clearly formulated analyses of their intelligence?"

"I can," replied the professor.

"I had better tell you," said the Dictator, "in order to avoid any misunderstanding, what I mean by intelligence."

"Do," said Professor Bl.

"I mean," the Dictator said, and as he picked his words, his face was suddenly that of a perplexed schoolboy; "I mean by it the ability to classify the phenomena of the world according to cause and effect."

"That is quite plausibly expressed," Professor Bl. said approvingly. The Dictator was delighted and the parting was amiable.

From that day on, wherever Professor Bl. came, went, or stopped still, there appeared obtrusive men wearing bowler hats who did their very utmost to seem unobtrusive but whom even the children always greeted with the words: "Good morning, Mr. Detective." They amused Professor Bl. mightily. They were the only people, except his wife, who could boast of being treated in a friendly manner by Professor Bl.

Soon afterwards the men who had by the Dictator's wish to submit to his analysis began to present themselves at the professor's laboratory. The process did not take long and was not painful; nevertheless these gentlemen did not all submit with a very good grace. The Dictator sent seven of them in all in the course of two weeks. The professor did his job and wrote down his formulæ with a brief and clear explanation. He transcribed the formulæ of six of them accurately, but that of the seventh he deliberately falsified.

A month later the Dictator sent for Professor Bl. a second time. This time his reception was official and pompous. The small, peevish professor was ushered up the monumental stairway of the castle with assiduous formality after running the gauntlet of salutes from the Dictator's picked guard. Then they were alone together and the formalities ceased. The Dictator was as cordial as ever.

"Why did you try to take me in with Analysis No. 7, Professor?" he asked with sly and jovial good humour, laughing pleasantly. Professor Bl. laughed too.

The newspapers published the result of the interview. The Dictator, they said, took the liveliest personal interest in Professor Bl.'s investigations. The Dictator had resolved to make a state monopoly of the scientist's activities for the good of the nation.

A commodious house and a superb laboratory were made

ready for the physiologist in the capital. The Minister of Education informed him in glittering terms that his services were of such importance to the state that he was on no account to leave the capital without first informing the Minister. The gentlemen in bowlers were increased by two.

Professor Bl.'s activities were not exhausting. Now and then people came along whose intelligence he had to analyse at the Dictator's request. What followed therefrom was known neither to the Professor nor to anyone else. It was considered a wry jest in the dictatorial circle when the Dictator sent anyone to be analysed, a subtle reprimand. "To send a man to Professor Bl.," became a catch-phrase throughout the country, having the meaning of a humorous, and sometimes also a serious, warning.

A year passed and another after that. The Dictator became an old hand at wielding all the attributes of power; there were only two other men on the planet as adroit as he. He had an efficient army, an excellent police force; every office and every key position in industry throughout the land were occupied by persons whose qualifications as adherents of his own were tested year by year. When he looked on what he had done he might say that he had done well. And yet the Dictator's sleep was not sound, for well as he had done he had not done as well as he wished. The truth was, things went well for his adherents, but not for the country; and his original intention had been that things should go well for everybody.

He paid more and more frequent visits to the physiologist, and found it scarcely more difficult than at first to treat him in a simple and human manner. He laughed a lot when he was with Professor Bl. No one who knew the Dictator only from his brazen mask had any idea how he could laugh. Professor Bl. laughed too. Probably the gentlemen in bowlers also laughed, for it may be assumed that from somewhere or other they listened in on the conversations.

One evening towards the close of the second year the Dictator dined with the professor. There was a silence after dinner which was broken by the professor's saying in his peevish, quizzical manner: "Just tell me straight out what you want with me. We've been playing hide-and-seek for two years now."

At this the Dictator frowned and came within an ace of showing the scientist the mailed fist; but he recovered himself just in time and maintained his simple and human manner. In the third year, one summer evening, when the professor's wife was away at a distant watering-place, the

Dictator said: "How would it be if you took an analysis of *my* intelligence."

Professor Bl. went a shade paler. "Has it come to that?" he replied.

"Don't you want to?" asked the Dictator.

"I do not," replied Professor Bl.

The Dictator looked at him, and never had he spoken as man to man with such cordiality. "After all, you can cheat," he said confidentially, with an encouraging smile.

"I don't think," replied the professor, and he too smiled until his large yellow teeth showed through his beard, "I don't think there would be much good in cheating. I think you would tumble to it."

So the professor made the analysis at the Dictator's wish. It did not take long, nor did it seem long to the Dictator, but then when he looked back it seemed to have taken very long, for in that space of time he had become young and then old, and then young and then old again. The professor said as little as possible while recording the measurements. He wrote down the formulæ on a sheet of paper. The formulæ were quite legible to the Dictator; he knew that they were written in small letters and figures and that there were twenty-three of them.

The professor wrote his last formula and gave the paper to the Dictator.

"Thank you," said the Dictator. He took the sheet, folded it unread, asked for an envelope, put the folded paper inside it, licked its flap, shook the professor's hand, and went away.

After his departure Professor Bl. felt slightly fatigued; yes, his legs were unpleasantly heavy and they trembled; but he did not think of sitting down to get his breath. On the contrary he paced up and down his laboratory, stroking his instruments, and finally he walked all through the house and then into the garden. Normally, if people came in, he found them an interruption and got rid of them as soon as he could. Today the house seemed very large and the garden very large, and both empty, terribly empty. He tried to telephone to his wife, to his assistants, but as it turned out he could not get in touch with any of them. He might have expected that. He would have been glad to exchange a word even with one of those obtrusive gentlemen in bowler hats, but even they were absent today.

Finally he came upon his old laboratory attendant. He had been with him now for twenty years and Professor Bl.

knew the man's skin, the composition of his blood, and the exact state of his heart and his kidneys. Today for the first time he inquired into his opinions. He asked him what he thought about God and the other world. It appeared that the laboratory attendant had thought a great deal about them. "I am a man made for belief," he said.

Professor Bl. was pleased by this remark. He found it straightforward and rational. Now he sat on the terrace, below which lay the garden, and his restlessness passed away. It would not be a bad idea to go for a walk through the streets; but then, he reflected, the bowler hats would be around and he had no longer any desire for their company. So he sat still. He thought of the people who had been with him in recent years, his wife, his assistants. They pleased him. He got on with them. He had even got on with the Dictator. The man acted according to his nature, though it was certainly going a bit far to want to have himself endorsed by himself.

That same evening, before his wife returned and before he had spoken to his assistants, Professor Bl. fell ill. The morning papers announced that the illness was serious, the evening papers that it was grave, and the morning after, before his wife saw him again, Professor Bl. was dead. The Dictator paid a visit in the course of the day and had hourly bulletins brought him.

The great scientist was buried with public honours and much pomp.

Two weeks later came the tenth anniversary of the day on which the Dictator had seized power. It was a day of great splendour; his enemies hated him with a peculiar and well-grounded hate, for they had little prospect now of attaining their ends. And many of them hated him merely because they might no longer hope to be his adherents. For he had closed the list of his adherents; there was so many that he didn't care to have any more.

Earlier, the Dictator had loved these days of great acclamation; they had been his support and endorsement. Now he went through them with a certain impatience; they were no more than political expedients which in his heart he no longer needed. He preferred the short interval in the early afternoon which he had to himself. He spent half this time in gymnastic exercises with his trainer, and then after being massaged he reclined alone in the small, cool room which contained only a couch, a writing-table, and an arm-chair and was entered by no one except one of his secretaries.

BRAIN SPECIALIST

He lay there exhausted, vacant, in an agreeable indolence, with nothing brazen about him. Words of command came up half muted from the square as detachments were marched up, ready to do him homage. In twenty-five minutes he had to appear on the balcony and make a speech; he had no idea what he would say, but he knew it would be the right thing and that loud-speakers would transmit his words throughout the world.

He got up. Enveloped in his wrap he walked across to the writing-table. There were mementoes locked up in it, a collection for his own eye only of foolish, trivial things. A few letters, a uniform button flattened by a bullet, an old photograph. He loved these mementoes and was happy to rummage about among them; he felt stronger when he was in physical contact with his earlier days.

He took out a key and then another key and then from a last and innermost drawer he pulled out a sealed envelope, just a fortnight old. He knew well what was in it. Perhaps it was only for the sake of this envelope he had gone to the writing-table.

He stood for minutes with the unopened envelope containing the formula of the dead professor in his hand. Then he picked up a slender paper-knife. It would be interesting to know what was in the envelope. Profit and wisdom—there were certain theories inside. Professor Bl., now dead, knew something about it; had just hinted at it. It might not have been impossible to get Professor Bl., now dead, to tell him more about it. The Dictator was no fool and the professor had allowed him talent. The logic of history had imposed power upon him and power makes people stupid. If he had not been a powerful man, who knows, he might have been a great one.

From below came the tumult of the crowd. Time to get dressed—in fourteen minutes he had to make his speech. It would assuredly do his speech no good if he knew the contents of the envelope. The Dictator put down the paper-knife unused, and tore the envelope and its contents into small pieces.

Then he walked through the large stateroom and out on to the balcony and made his speech.